WIND-GONE-MAD

SELECTED FICTION WORKS BY L. RON HUBBARD

FANTASY

The Case of the Friendly Corpse

Death's Deputy

Fear

The Ghoul

The Indigestible Triton

Slaves of Sleep & The Masters of Sleep

Typewriter in the Sky

The Ultimate Adventure

SCIENCE FICTION

Battlefield Earth

The Conquest of Space

The End Is Not Yet

Final Blackout

The Kilkenny Cats

The Kingslayer

The Mission Earth Dekalogy*

Ole Doc Methuselah

To the Stars

ADVENTURE

The Hell Job series

WESTERN

Buckskin Brigades

Empty Saddles

Guns of Mark Jardine

Hot Lead Payoff

A full list of L. Ron Hubbard's
novellas and short stories is provided at the back.

*Dekalogy—a group of ten volumes

WIND-GONE-MAD

Published by
Galaxy Press, LLC
7051 Hollywood Boulevard, Suite 200
Hollywood, CA 90028

Printed in the United States of America.

ISBN-10 1-59212-269-8
ISBN-13 978-1-59212-269-1

Library of Congress Control Number: 2007903528

CONTENTS

STORIES FROM PULP FICTION'S GOLDEN AGE

A ND it *was* a golden age. The 1930s and 1940s were a vibrant, seminal time for a gigantic audience of eager readers, probably the largest per capita audience of readers in American history. The magazine racks were chock-full of publications with ragged trims, garish cover art, cheap brown pulp paper, low cover prices—and the most excitement you could hold in your hands.

"Pulp" magazines, named for their rough-cut, pulpwood paper, were a vehicle for more amazing tales than Scheherazade could have told in a million and one nights. Set apart from higher-class "slick" magazines, printed on fancy glossy paper with quality artwork and superior production values, the pulps were for the "rest of us," adventure story after adventure story for people who liked to *read*. Pulp fiction authors were no-holds-barred entertainers—real storytellers. They were more interested in a thrilling plot twist, a horrific villain or a white-knuckle adventure than they were in lavish prose or convoluted metaphors.

The sheer volume of tales released during this wondrous golden age remains unmatched in any other period of literary history—hundreds of thousands of published stories in over nine hundred different magazines. Some titles lasted only an issue or two; many magazines succumbed to paper shortages during World War II, while others endured for decades yet. Pulp fiction remains as a treasure trove of stories you can read, stories you can love, stories you can remember. The stories were driven by plot and character, with grand heroes, terrible villains, beautiful damsels (often in distress), diabolical plots, amazing places, breathless romances. The readers wanted to be taken beyond the mundane, to live adventures far removed from their ordinary lives—and the pulps rarely failed to deliver.

In that regard, pulp fiction stands in the tradition of all memorable literature. For as history has shown, good stories are much more than fancy prose. William Shakespeare, Charles Dickens, Jules Verne, Alexandre Dumas—many of the greatest literary figures wrote their fiction for the readers, not simply literary colleagues and academic admirers. And writers for pulp magazines were no exception. These publications reached an audience that dwarfed the circulations of today's short story magazines. Issues of the pulps were scooped up and read by over thirty million avid readers each month.

Because pulp fiction writers were often paid no more than a cent a word, they had to become prolific or starve. They also had to write aggressively. As Richard Kyle, publisher and editor of *Argosy,* the first and most long-lived of the pulps, so pointedly explained: "The pulp magazine writers, the best of them, worked for markets that did not write for critics or attempt to satisfy timid advertisers. Not having to answer to anyone other than their readers, they wrote about human beings on the edges of the unknown, in those new lands the future would explore. They wrote for what we would become, not for what we had already been."

Some of the more lasting names that graced the pulps include H. P. Lovecraft, Edgar Rice Burroughs, Robert E. Howard, Max Brand, Louis L'Amour, Elmore Leonard, Dashiell Hammett, Raymond Chandler, Erle Stanley Gardner, John D. MacDonald, Ray Bradbury, Isaac Asimov, Robert Heinlein—and, of course, L. Ron Hubbard.

In a word, he was among the most prolific and popular writers of the era. He was also the most enduring—hence this series—and certainly among the most legendary. It all began only months after he first tried his hand at fiction, with L. Ron Hubbard tales appearing in *Thrilling Adventures, Argosy, Five-Novels Monthly, Detective Fiction Weekly, Top-Notch, Texas Ranger, War Birds, Western Stories,* even *Romantic Range.* He could write on any subject, in any genre, from jungle explorers to deep-sea divers, from G-men and gangsters, cowboys and flying aces to mountain climbers, hard-boiled detectives and spies. But he really began to shine when he turned his talent to science fiction and fantasy of which he authored nearly fifty novels or novelettes to forever change the shape of those genres.

Following in the tradition of such famed authors as Herman Melville, Mark Twain, Jack London and Ernest Hemingway, Ron Hubbard actually lived adventures that his own characters would have admired—as an ethnologist among primitive tribes, as prospector and engineer in hostile climes, as a captain of vessels on four oceans. He even wrote a series of articles for *Argosy*, called "Hell Job," in which he lived and told of the most dangerous professions a man could put his hand to.

Finally, and just for good measure, he was also an accomplished photographer, artist, filmmaker, musician and educator. But he was first and foremost a *writer*, and that's the L. Ron Hubbard we come to know through the pages of this volume.

This library of Stories from the Golden Age presents the best of L. Ron Hubbard's fiction from the heyday of storytelling, the Golden Age of the pulp magazines. In these eighty volumes, readers are treated to a full banquet of 153 stories, a kaleidoscope of tales representing every imaginable genre: science fiction, fantasy, western, mystery, thriller, horror, even romance—action of all kinds and in all places.

Because the pulps themselves were printed on such inexpensive paper with high acid content, issues were not meant to endure. As the years go by, the original issues of every pulp from *Argosy* through *Zeppelin Stories* continue crumbling into brittle, brown dust. This library preserves the L. Ron Hubbard tales from that era, presented with a distinctive look that brings back the nostalgic flavor of those times.

L. Ron Hubbard's Stories from the Golden Age has something for every taste, every reader. These tales will return you to a time when fiction was good clean entertainment and the most fun a kid could have on a rainy afternoon or the best thing an adult could enjoy after a long day at work. Pick up a volume, and remember what reading is supposed to be all about. Remember curling up with a *great story*.

—Kevin J. Anderson

KEVIN J. ANDERSON *is the author of more than ninety critically acclaimed works of speculative fiction, including The Saga of Seven Suns, the continuation of the Dune Chronicles with Brian Herbert, and his* New York Times *bestselling novelization of L. Ron Hubbard's* Ai! Pedrito!

WIND-GONE-MAD

CHAPTER ONE

A GAINST a sky the color of a chalk-smudged slate, there appeared a black cotton ball which vanished as swiftly as it had come. In its place, long black lines came into being, disappearing in their turn. These were warnings only. The next markers of potential death would be much closer to the sleek biplane which rode the China sky.

The man called Feng-Feng, "Wind-Gone-Mad," looked down and smiled with half his mouth. He eased back his stick and jumped another thousand feet into the glowering sky. Once more he gave the landscape a careful scrutiny.

Below and ahead lay the town of Taiy of the Shan Province, sprawling out like the yellow toy blocks of a child, hemmed on two sides by the craggy Khinghan Mountains, split apart by the golden Y which marked the Fen Ho River and its two northernmost tributaries.

Another puff—near this time—spread itself out into oblivion. The black streaks of tracer machine-gun bullets did not reach this high. The man called Wind-Gone-Mad jockeyed his slim fighting craft abruptly out of range and scanned the terrain for the landing field of North China Airways.

Evidently, they did not know him, and to land meant a shattering baptism of fire. But land he must. Both gas gauge and mission demanded that. Wind-Gone-Mad angled down in a screeching power dive, and wondered what the admirals would say if they could witness this reception in "peaceable Northern China."

Yesterday, a representative of the great Amalgamated Aeronautical Co.—Jim Dahlgren—sat across a mirrorlike table from the military powers that rule China's destinies. Before them were scattered squares of cheap yellow paper which bore messages marked "Urgent." Arms bedecked with gold braid picked them up. Lips accustomed to bawling orders on a quarterdeck spoke hushed words.

"It comes," the C-in-C of the USN muttered, "it comes of letting the implements of war wander into the unscrupulous hands of power-crazed men. With three bombing planes, 'The Butcher' is of the opinion that he can rule all China. Gentlemen, it must be stopped."

"Stopped!" the British officer echoed. "Rather. But how? We cannot land armed forces. Such would be regarded as an antagonistic move against the Japanese along the border."

"I appreciate that," the Italian officer clipped. "But perhaps if we were to advise B-34 to kill The Butcher at all costs—"

The Frenchman growled deep in his many-chinned throat. "Murder! Bah! We cannot stoop to that. Besides, my dear Gian, The Butcher has repelled such attacks before."

And then the Chinese adviser to the council of nations unexpectedly uttered an opinion. "As the gods of war will have it, let it rest. Before this, men like The Butcher have risen up in the provinces with fire and sword. The Butcher has purchased his three bombers. He has decreed that Shen

Province is at war with Shan Province. Nothing will stop his conquest because without additional taxes, The Butcher's administration is at end. After all, I say, it has happened before. In a few years, The Butcher will most likely die or be killed. It is best to wait for that which is decreed by the gods—"

Eyes raked him scornfully—Western eyes, unhampered by fatalism.

The man called Jim Dahlgren stood up and wiped blond hair out of light-gray eyes. His lips were tight in a sardonic smile. "There is, as you say, a brand of diplomacy." He waited until all of them gave their attention. "That brand is called eye for an eye. Force must be met with force."

The C-in-C muttered, "Men like you profit by that. Sit down, Dahlgren. You want to sell Shan Province a fleet of bombers. We will not have it. That is the only solution to you—the one which will put dollars in your pocket. Sit down."

But Dahlgren remained on his feet, still smiling. "No, I was not thinking of that. There is a man called Feng-Feng—Wind-Gone-Mad—"

"You know him?" bawled the C-in-C with unexpected heat. "That pirate! If you do, tell us where we can find him. The United States will be only too glad to pay you for your trouble."

Dahlgren shrugged and his lean face was hard. "Yes. I imagine that you would, all of you. In your hearts you know what he wants and you also want it. He stands for a unified China. A China without civil war. A China which can resist invasion from without and treason from within. You will

5

not let others of us interfere with politics. We must sell only when a buyer comes to us. But Wind-Gone-Mad knows who should buy and he sees that they come unhampered when they need defense. He has studied this country for years and he knows better than you who have been here months."

Dahlgren reached for his soft felt hat. "I go now to find the one they call Wind-Gone-Mad."

"I forbid you to contact that man!" bawled the C-in-C. But it was the official who spoke and not the man. He watched Dahlgren go out and heard the staccato heel beats going down the corridor.

The Italian's eyes went up to the smoke-clouded ceiling. "Well," he remarked to the room at large, "I for one am glad. This Feng-Feng, after all, *has* done things in the past—"

But that was yesterday, and today the man called Wind-Gone-Mad lanced down toward the airways field, finding a reason to smile. Instead of antiaircraft guns, Taiy was using ancient 75s and a quantity of bluff.

The square of yellow earth slid up over the motor cowl with appalling speed. The altimeter shot down to five hundred feet before the pilot whipped his ship into a slashing sideslip.

Men in gray uniforms were running away from deserted machine guns, disappearing behind piles of sandbags. An officer stopped to empty his automatic at the charging slash of color.

The pilot fishtailed wildly and shot over the stiff windsock. The plane snapped suddenly into landing position. With a crunching slap, the ship was down.

It was as if an electric current had been shut off. Men began to fumble for their lost caps. Gunners slouched back to their pieces. The officer calmly slid another clip into his gun and holstered it. On the side of the red fuselage they had all seen the dragon and the two mammoth characters which identified their visitor. They knew this man and they also knew that he had little connection with The Butcher.

The pilot stood up in his narrow pit and stretched. But he did not remove the goggles which hid a quarter of his face, nor did he so much as unfasten the chin strap of the lurid helmet he wore.

The officer, a White Russian, stopped and looked at the red dragon which spat fire above the pilot's eyes and then curled down around the ear pads. Assured of the man's identity, he came forward again.

"I am sorry, Feng-Feng. Had I but seen the dragon—"

"Quite all right," interrupted the pilot. "I wish an audience with Cheng-Wang immediately."

"Cheng-Wang is at your service, I am sure. But perhaps it would be better for us to place your plane in a bombproof hangar. We are waiting an attack by The Butcher. Perhaps if we service your engine, when the bombers come you can—"

Wind-Gone-Mad laughed joyously. "Such faith! You think that I would attack three Demming bombers single-handed? Really, my good friend Blakely sells better ships than you suppose. I would be downed in an instant."

It was the Russian's turn to laugh. Wind-Gone-Mad shot down? The thing was impossible, ludicrous. In a moment he subsided and spoke again more seriously. "Had Cheng-Wang listened better to the proposition to buy three Amalgamated bombers when you asked—"

"Quiet," said Feng-Feng, not unkindly. "That is a secret that only a few of us hold. Its release would mean my death. But never mind. I go to see Cheng-Wang. Service my ship and listen in on my panel radio for talk in Shen Province. The pigs will give you warning. If you know that they come, send for me and I will do my best to beat them off." He dropped to the ground lightly and strode toward a waiting motorcycle.

Cheng-Wang was old. On his parchment face was stamped the weariness of one who has seen too much, has fought too many battles, has witnessed too often the summer's fading into the dusty harshness of winter.

Cheng-Wang was frail and when he moved his hands the almost-fleshless bones clattered above the click of his long fingernails. With an impassive nod, he gave the order that the man called Feng-Feng be admitted to the audience room.

Still masked by his goggles and casqued by his helmet, Wind-Gone-Mad entered with long, determined strides. His leather flying coat rustled when he sat down in the indicated chair.

"It pleases me that you come," said Cheng-Wang in five-toned Mandarin Chinese. "Long have I wanted to give you my regrets for not accepting your offer and your warning. Now there is little we can do. The Butcher has begun his fight and it will be short. Along the eastern border, my troops lose miles of ground each day. They are harassed from the air. But you have come too late."

Behind the lenses of the great goggles, Feng-Feng's gray eyes held those of the provincial governor. "I do not think that I have. Our friend Blakely sold them no pursuit planes because they could procure no pilots. At the North China Airways field I now have a fighting ship—my own. It has two machine guns and it travels four miles a minute. With that I can help you."

"It is useless," mourned Cheng-Wang. "I will not allow you to throw your life to The Butcher. You do it out of sympathy alone and you use no regard for your own safety. The Butcher has placed a price on you, and that long ago. He would see your helmeted head dangling from a picket. Blakely, the man you oddly call your friend, negotiated that these many months gone by."

"There are no bombers at my call in Shanghai," stated the man called Feng-Feng. "I can only do as fate and my hand dictate. Is it true that you are to receive an air attack today?"

Without explanation, knowing that it was not needed, Cheng-Wang presented a square of paper which bore black slashes. Deciphered, it said:

> The Hawks of The Butcher strike before dark. It is better to accept an honorable surrender from Cheng-Wang than for The Butcher to occupy a lifeless town.

The massive black doors swung back and a soldier in gray stood rigidly at attention in the opening. He saluted. "To the east, heaven-borne, are the Hawks of The Butcher." Dropping his hand he left-faced, waiting for Wind-Gone-Mad to precede him out of the palace.

The pilot turned, and his mouth was set. "Refuse to know terror, Cheng-Wang. This one goes to dull the claws of The Butcher." He tramped rapidly away and the black doors swung softly shut behind him.

Chapter Two

WITH four chill miles of air sliding over his cowl each passing minute, Wind-Gone-Mad flew east and south. Earphones were snapped down over his helmet and he wrote with his right hand on a white pad while he flew dexterously with his left.

Out on the murky horizon, three short pencil lines against the gray heralded the approach of the bombers. They were headed for Taiy, engines yowling, bellies abristle with finned death.

Twenty-seven tons of demolition bombs, eighteen skilled Chinese, twelve six-hundred-and-fifty horsepower engines. They were the pride of The Butcher and the handiwork of Demming Aeronautical Corporation. Better than half a million dollars, they had cost, and the salesman—Blakely—had pocketed a ten percent commission. The Butcher had found them to be cheap at the price.

The man called Wind-Gone-Mad closed his writing pad and nodded tightly to himself. The bombers were keeping in constant contact with their radio station in Sing. They ran no chance of an unexpected attack from the air. That much was easily gleaned from their ticking chatter. They were not quite at ease concerning the lack of war equipment in Shan. It seemed too simple. They had only to drop their bombs to lay Taiy out in crumbled, smoldering rubble. In Sing, The Butcher himself was beside the key urging them on.

The pursuit ship pilot scowled thoughtfully at his instruments and then opened the pad once more. On it he jotted a rapid calculation. He himself had been fifty minutes in the air and was now two hundred miles from Taiy and on the route to Sing.

The distance between the two capitals could be completed in another fifty minutes, whereas it would require the bombers about a hundred and thirty minutes to complete their run to Taiy.

The earphones were crackling again, stridently. Incongruously, the words were in English and the code was International Morse. That came from the impossibility of reducing Chinese ideographs to dots and dashes. No code was used because English was foreign enough to these operators without complicating the words themselves.

The incessant buzzing had warned the Russian of the bombers' departure from Sing and it was now giving Wind-Gone-Mad the germ of an idea.

Like the hurricane his name represented, the pilot nosed up and shot skyward a thousand feet. He was above the bombers now, in position for an attack. He could look down into cockpits which seemed to spew machine guns. He could see goggles flash in the afternoon sunlight and knew that they were watching him. They could see that dragon on his fuselage and the characters which were his name. Abruptly, he declared war.

Coming like a blood-steeped javelin, the pilot aimed straight for the nose of the lead ship. Six separate sets of lines clawed out at him from nervously blossoming muzzles.

He pressed his own trips and his belts began to eat through. Smoking cartridges tumbled back into his slipstream. Cordite cut knifelike into his lungs. Under him, the bombers spread like a landing field, sliding up at him in a shimmering blur through his prop.

He swooped into a zoom, went over the hump, and slashed down at the second bomber. His guns were chattering madly and the sky all about him was gray with tracer smoke. Like jagged, red lightning, he went under the plane's great belly, sliced back in a loop and sent a sizzling salvo into the upper wing of the third ship.

Pulling back, he jumped his altimeter needle up two thousand feet before he looked back down. The formation below was a little ragged, but the mammoth planes were plodding stolidly along toward Taiy. Goggles were flashing while observers watched him.

His gray eyes narrow, Wind-Gone-Mad threw in the switch on his own small but complete broadcasting set and reeled out a short section of whipping antenna. His index finger clipped the key in a rapid series of dots and dashes.

First he sent out his own title, in English: "Wind-Gone-Mad." After that, in a rush so swift that only an expert could hope to receive it, he sent out the date of his birth, the distance to the moon and the horsepower of his engine. He then adjusted his earphones and threw the switch back. He knew very well that

Coming like a blood-steeped javelin, the pilot aimed straight for the nose of the lead ship. Six separate sets of lines clawed out at him from nervously blossoming muzzles.

he had given a sizable imitation of a code message and that the three bomber operators and the men down in Sing would pull out their beards in an attempt to decipher something not decipherable.

Smiling tightly, Wind-Gone-Mad headed once more south and east toward Sing. Behind him, three puzzled bombers lumbered on and filled the air with excited dots and dashes, trying to reassure each other, trying to contact The Butcher.

But The Butcher's orders were to the point. "Proceed to Taiy and bomb it into oblivion. If Wind-Gone-Mad comes here, he will find exquisite death." And then a remark evidently directed to the pursuit ship's pilot, "You hear that, pirate?"

Wind-Gone-Mad slipped in his switch and rattled his own key: "I hear. I am coming. Tie on your ears, Butcher, for I may wish to string them into a necklace and give them to Cheng-Wang."

After that, the yellow landscape crept by three thousand feet below and the shadows began to slant, assuming incredible lengths. Wind-Gone-Mad flew calmly south and east and waited until fifty minutes had been ticked off on the face of his panel clock.

Below, a river came into being, its snaky length shimmering. Behind that climbed Sing, built, seemingly, in steps up the side of a mountain—vanguard of the sullen range beyond. It was easy to pick out The Butcher's palace, and easier still to select the riverside square which served as a landing field.

But they had been waiting for the pursuit ship. Blakely was too good a salesman to sell aircraft without selling antiaircraft guns. From the heights of the city a clump of squat trees suddenly shrouded themselves with flame and smoke. From the top of a concrete warehouse, carelessly piled sandbags erupted, swarming with men. At both ends of the field, machine-gun crews went to work with weapons which had been equipped with special sights.

Wind-Gone-Mad barrel rolled, looped, barrel rolled again and then confined his defense to jockeying his rudders.

His gray eyes were without expression, almost disinterested. He had the air of a man who idly watches the antics of a bug. Wind-Gone-Mad knew that it takes time to prepare gun crews and The Butcher had not had that time.

But he had to go down, and when he did, the machine guns would get in their work. That decided, the pilot dived for a hundred feet, pulled over into a loop and straightened out. Looking up, he saw the ground. Where he should have been, a black cloud was sending out a thousand angry hornets. The archy gunners were doing a better job of speed calculation.

His next maneuver carried him straight down. His outraged engine bellowed shrilly, shaking the ground below. The top of the warehouse began to leap up and expand. The gunners on its roof were suddenly paralyzed, unable to move.

Two converging streams of blue tracers lashed down, probing, sending spurts of dust out of the sandbags. A machine gunner raised his piece bodily away from its mount and staggered back. The water jacket was suddenly gashed, pouring out its rusty life fluid. The gunner released the grip and clutched at his throat.

The gunners on its roof were suddenly paralyzed,
unable to move.

A trail of white specks went along the gray cement, eating up men and guns, seeming to hammer the bullets back into the blazing snouts of the weapons.

Over on his back again, he was streaking upside down for the field. They hadn't expected him to go that way. The other path was suddenly ripped by exploding shrapnel. Wind-Gone-Mad snap rolled and lanced toward a small white building at one edge of the flying field. He had seen the cage formed by radio wires and his earphones no longer snapped.

Under him, a yellow two-seater huddled on the line. The pilot needed no second glance to identify the ship. On its side was painted the triangle and bar of Demming Aircraft. That meant that Blakely was here.

The small white hut was no longer small. It loomed like a mansion through the ring sight. The pilot caught sight of something else. A row of gas drums stood fatly against the white wall, evidently because of the shelter afforded there from the sun.

Wind-Gone-Mad rapidly shifted his plans. He streaked out across the river, out of range, dwindling from sight like a golf ball on a three-hundred-yard drive. Amazed, the Chinese gunners followed his movements with suspicion.

The pilot reached into his bullet rack and pulled out a metal case marked with the red stripe which signified incendiary ammunition. With an expert flip of his wrist he loaded his right-hand gun. Another case, another load, and Wind-Gone-Mad slashed air in a swift turn. Twenty feet above the ground, four miles a minute, he scorched the grass tops with the blast of his exhaust.

Once more the shack jumped into the sight. Wind-Gone-Mad pressed gently on his rudder. He eased his stick back an immeasurable fraction of an inch. Trips down, he gave the first drum in the row a double line of raw fire. The second drum, the third, fourth, fifth, and then back on the stick, leaping into the fading sky with bullets gnawing like riveters at his wings and fuselage.

Black puffs darkened the dusk about him. Shrapnel sang off his struts. His stick jerked and a hole appeared jaggedly in the right aileron. The world dipped, swept back, dipped again. The altimeter needle read five thousand feet.

Safe for the moment, Wind-Gone-Mad found time to look back along his tail at the ground. Down there, ants were running away from a fire which shot red and blue flame a hundred feet into the air. The radio shack was going and going fast. A mast tottered and fell, showering sparks over half an acre. The gas drums, whether empty or full, had exploded. Half the work was done.

Wind-Gone-Mad found a moment to smile. He unreeled his antenna, threw in the broadcasting switch and tuned his dials. With his finger on the key he pursed his lips in composition. Then, with a nod, he clattered his key. He still had thirty minutes to stop the bombing of Taiy.

Dash, dash, dot, dash, dot, dot, dot, dash, said the key. *Dash, dash, dot, dash, dot, dot, dot, dash.* "QST QST. Calling bomber pilots. Calling bomber pilots."

Wind-Gone-Mad listened in for a moment and when he had heard the stuttering, hurried answer, he threw his switch, threw his power on full, and rattled his key again.

INTELLIGENCE JUST RECEIVED TEN PURSUIT PLANES WAITING TAIY. AMBUSH WAITING YOU AT TAIY. DO NOT ATTACK. DO NOT ATTACK. AMBUSH WAITING YOU. RETURN THIS FIELD IMMEDIATELY TO AID IN REPELLING ATTACKING PURSUIT PLANE PILOTED BY WIND-GONE-MAD. RETURN THIS FIELD IMMEDIATELY. DISOBEDIENCE IS DEATH. SIGNED, THE BUTCHER.

A mad clatter came back through the earphones. Three keys were asking three thousand questions. Wind-Gone-Mad cut through once, severely. After that the keys were still for a full minute. Three separate messages came back, each the same.

"Returning," radioed the bombers.

Wind-Gone-Mad took time out to smile and felt that he owed it to himself. He was climbing now and he reeled in his antenna. The Butcher had lost a point. Without the radio shack he could not communicate with his planes, and the pilot was certain that he had destroyed the only broadcasting station in the province.

The bombers had intended to attack Taiy at dusk, but now dusk had come with long black patches on the fading ground and the bombs still nestled close to the giant bellies.

But this, Wind-Gone-Mad told himself, was only a breathing space. Tomorrow the bombers would go back and Cheng-Wang would be governor of shambles. Tomorrow, The Butcher would plan greater things. Next week, next month, next year, The Butcher would spread his web over China, and Demming Aeronautical Co. would grow rich with selling the winged implements of war.

Nothing the admirals could do would stop it. They would sit back and dictate lengthy explanations. They could not land troops for yet a while for there was still Japan. Perhaps The Butcher entertained large ideas about Manchuria.

A pilot in a sleek, red plane adjusted his goggles and thought about the course of nations, wondering at the best plan, juggling destiny at four miles a minute.

Darkness was spreading out like a black sheet, torn and unraveled. The east glowed briefly red, shed a few stray shafts on the mountain tips, and then all light was gone.

The pilot cut his engine and glided sibilantly down to where the river snaked a silver band beside the hills. Photographed on his mind were two particular bends, for between them lay a flat expanse which might be used as a field.

Wires singing softly, Wind-Gone-Mad felt for the ground with his wheels, slipped to kill excess speed, mushed, and then crunched in for a landing.

He listened for a moment and climbed down. Satisfied that he had not been observed, he reached into his engine and ripped out a gas line. Working with a wrench he unfastened the carburetor and kneeled, burying the metal deep in the soft ground under the nose. Destroying all traces of the cache, Wind-Gone-Mad made certain that his goggles were still in place and that his helmet strap was tight.

With a set jaw and an amused expression in his gray eyes, he slipped softly into the darkness toward the town of Sing. He had four hours before the bombers returned.

Chapter Three

FROM down across the Gobi the chill night wind was blowing, probing into guttering street lanterns, running icy fingers up and down the backs of cotton-clad men, whispering doleful tidings through the closed shutters of houses.

The Wei River gave off a ghostlike mist which insinuated itself through the steplike streets, blanketing the thick gray dust beneath a clinging coat of mud.

Alleys loomed like deep mysterious caverns. Shop doorways were murky yellow lights thwarted by fog. Head and shoulders above all else, the palace of The Butcher reared its cold, clammy face.

Wind-Gone-Mad sought the darkness; his boots were soundless. Wraithlike, he hugged the walls, a shadow against the shadows like an evil spirit come up from the river to seek its revenge. Of the few huddled, shuffling people that saw him, there was none who would admit the sight.

Deeply ingrained was their fear and belief in water devils, and during these days of savage reign and relentless conquest, a wise man was wise only when he saw nothing, said nothing, and heard nothing.

A gray-gowned Chinese, retreating home before the fog, swiftly passed an alleyway, but not quite swiftly enough. A strong, gripping hand snapped out and caught at his shoulder, a hard palm slapped back and stifled the scream which rose from the throat.

"Quiet," breathed Wind-Gone-Mad from the blackness. "This one searches out the foreign devil of the sky."

The Chinese felt the palm loosen slightly against his mouth. Cautiously, in a low voice, he imparted the information which this doubtless powerful water devil required.

"The foreign devil of the sky stays at his room in the Wagon-Lit. May the water devil walk in peace to the graves of his ancestors."

The palm was suddenly released, the arm withdrawn, and the Chinese stood very still for a full minute. Then a door swung open across the street, emitting a feeble shaft of yellow light and a low murmur of voices. Covertly, the Chinese glanced back to where the water devil had been. Quite naturally, there was nothing there. Running in zigzags to thwart any attempt at pursuit, the Chinese disappeared into the fog.

Wind-Gone-Mad made his way through the filth-strewn alleys to the back of the indicated hotel. He was pleased that Blakely was not quartered at the palace. Perhaps Blakely had not wanted to be too near The Butcher, for The Butcher's black rages were habitual and swift and unreasoning.

The Wagon-Lit was not an imposing structure, but in a city where one-story buildings were the rule, its double row of windows made it a prince among paupers. Its walls were grimy with the insistent bombardment of dust, worn and cracked with repeated freezes.

A dry-goods box crammed with trash stood forlornly at the back entrance. Wind-Gone-Mad eyed it and then looked up at the rooms on the second floor. Only one window was lighted and that, if his luck held, would contain Blakely of Demming Aircraft. Wind-Gone-Mad noted the narrow ledge outside the window and nodded with satisfaction.

From the box he went to the top of the slightly open door. From there he swung himself up to a precarious footing on the ledge. With the quick, sure steps of a cat, he crept along until he stood outside the lighted square.

Yes, his luck was holding. The wide-tailored back of a gray topcoat was toward him and only one man would wear such clothes in this country—Blakely. He was in the act of picking a soft felt hat from the dresser top.

Wind-Gone-Mad slipped out a stubby automatic and clicked off the safety. He reached into his pocket and pulled out a glove which he donned. Once more he stared through the glass. Between Wind-Gone-Mad and Blakely there was a reflection. It showed a glinting pair of goggles which gave the appearance of a monster's cruel eyes. It showed a square jaw almost black with cordite smoke and spattered oil. It showed a vicious dragon spitting flame just above the eyes.

Wind-Gone-Mad raised his hand and slashed out the glass with his gun muzzle. His voice was gentle, almost purring. "Good evening, Mr. Blakely. Don't leave because I am here."

Blakely whirled. The hand which held the hat was shaking badly. His face, however, was calm, with a trace of sullenness.

His voice was gentle, almost purring. "Good evening, Mr. Blakely. Don't leave because I am here."

The black eyes bore a flat expression. Motionless for a moment, Blakely shrugged, laid down his hat and gave his topcoat collar a twitch so that it stood up around his pointed ears. His mouth was drawn down at both corners and barely moved when he spoke.

"Wind-Gone-Mad," breathed Blakely. But there was no trace of terror in his words. It was merely a statement of indisputable fact.

A pair of mammoth, glinting eyes peered through the shattered glass. A blackened face was set and hard. The blue automatic hurled back the yellow rays of the feeble lamp. The red dragon hurled out its painted fire. Splinters crunched under foot when Wind-Gone-Mad stepped through.

"Sit down, Blakely. You look weary."

Blakely backed cautiously to an armed wicker chair and slumped into it. Once more he tugged at his topcoat collar, for the wind sweeping into the blasted window was cold.

"What do you want?" muttered Blakely.

"Several things. But first I would like to remark on your idiocy in selling The Butcher his planes. Not ethical at all. Didn't I warn you once before?"

"Not ethical, perhaps, but I made money. Incidentally, do you happen to know the risk you run? The Butcher has set a price on your head for tying up his war last fall, and if you should happen to be caught—well, it would be too bad."

"Why warn me?" purred Wind-Gone-Mad from the center of the rug.

Blakely shrugged. "I'm not quite that bad. Besides, torture

of anyone makes me a little sick, and I'd be honor-bound to witness it."

"I see. But you happen to be perfectly willing to see an entire province ruined by three of your big ships. It doesn't jibe, Blakely. Did you ever meet Cheng-Wang?"

"Once or twice."

"And you know that he runs a fair government. His taxes are not high. Rather than crush his people he had kept his army at actual policing strength. He did not want to burden his merchants by making them subscribe to a plane fund. And you sit there and tell me that a little torture makes you sick. You've seen aerial attacks, Blakely, and you know what they mean. Remember Chapei?"

Blakely nodded glumly, his eyes sullen. "But business is business. I'm not like Jim Dahlgren. I can't parley this lingo well enough to indulge in high-power sales talks."

"Jim Dahlgren," said Wind-Gone-Mad crisply, "is always certain that his planes will not be used for civil war. He's trying to shoot square with the Chinese. Jim knows a friend when he sees one."

"I wonder."

"You know he does. This little foray of yours is going to cost Demming Aircraft a pile of prestige."

"Why worry about my prestige?"

"Because we've all shouldered a part of the white man's burden in the unification of China and we all have to carry it well."

"The white man's burden! Hokum. I suppose you're keeping it up with this piracy of yours."

"Piracy?"

For the first time, Blakely showed signs of animation. "Yes," he gritted, "piracy. You attack all provinces, all nations indiscriminately. You're flying the jolly roger and when you get caught, you'll be beheaded like a river pirate."

He leaned back with a smirk. "And your old friend Dahlgren. There's a pal. His record is fine until he comes over here. Then he starts out handing you pay checks out of the sales you get for him."

The oval lenses glinted and the cordite blackened jaw was belligerent. "Jim Dahlgren has only one thing in mind. He wants a unified China. A China which can resist all attacks from without and can protect itself from propaganda from within. He and I are of the same mind."

"Don't try to pull that with me, Feng-Feng. Jim Dahlgren wants to sell Amalgamated planes. That's all. And you want to draw your pay. You're both the same as me, only I'm not such a grease-smooth talker."

Wind-Gone-Mad smiled, and the effect, heightened by the glinting goggles, was ghoulish. "Have you any idea of what can happen to you?"

The eyes were no longer sullen. The black light of terror began to seep across Blakely's face. In a moment, he once more had himself under control. "Yes, I know. You could put me in bad with the powers that be in Shanghai. You could ruin my reputation with the warlords. You could see to it that I disappear." He tugged once more at his collar. "But you won't."

"Perhaps not, if you are wise. Listen to me: You know that it is difficult for a Westerner to tell one Chinese from another."

"What's that got to do with it?"

Wind-Gone-Mad smiled. "And that it is just as difficult for a Chinese to tell one Westerner from another."

Sudden comprehension made Blakely sink deep into his chair. "Go on."

"And if you were to be found wandering about in unusual clothes—like these I have on—you would probably be taken prisoner, herded into a torture chamber and killed as Feng-Feng before you could ever prove that you were Blakely."

Blakely squirmed and knew that Wind-Gone-Mad was right.

"Take off your topcoat, Blakely."

Once more Blakely tugged at his coat collar, but this time, with the speed of a conjurer, his right hand plunged under his left armpit and in the next instant he held a gun. The muzzle swept up in a vicious, blurred arc.

Wind-Gone-Mad did not seem to move. Suddenly he was no longer in the center of the rug. He was beside Blakely's chair. His automatic muzzle slapped down on Blakely's wrist; his left hand went into Blakely's jaw. With a resigned clatter, the gun slipped to the floor and Blakely sagged in the wicker chair, his eyes far back in his skull.

Without wasting any more time than it took to assure himself that Blakely was unconscious, Wind-Gone-Mad went to work.

From a suitcase he extracted Blakely's helmet and goggles. Fully as large as his own, the eye protectors were tinted. The ear tabs on both sides bore the triangle and bar of Demming

Aircraft, yellow against the black leather. Sweeping off his own gray-and-red casque, Wind-Gone-Mad donned Blakely's, pulling the goggles down over his eyes.

Peeling off the topcoat, Wind-Gone-Mad substituted his own flying jacket on Blakely's back. Finding an extra pair of tailored pants, he put them on, dressing Blakely in the breeches and boots Wind-Gone-Mad had lately worn.

Before five minutes had elapsed, to all appearances, Blakely stood helmeted and goggled in the middle of the rug and Wind-Gone-Mad sprawled senseless in a chair.

Wind-Gone-Mad smiled with satisfaction. The topcoat fitted snugly and looked well. Blakely's shoes were not too tight. Blakely's dark scarf partially hid Feng-Feng's chin. Wind-Gone-Mad looked in the mirror and then discovered again that his face was almost black. He spent a moment in washing and then found shoe polish which he mixed with the dust in the room corners. This he smeared on Blakely's sagging jaw, standing back to admire the effect.

The Demming man's trunk stood in the corner, its rope snarled about its base, but not for long. In a moment it was under Blakely's arms and Blakely himself was being lowered gently down to the shadow-steeped alley.

Wind-Gone-Mad tied the end of the rope, pocketed what papers he could find, and then he, too, stood in the alley. He cut the rope and shook Blakely back to consciousness.

In the darkness, Blakely's voice was thick. "Turn on the light."

"Quiet," breathed Wind-Gone-Mad. "Feel your clothes,

your face, your boots. To a Chinese, and maybe even to a Westerner, you look like me—enough anyway to fool men who have not often seen me."

"For heaven's sake!" hissed Blakely. "It's murder."

"If you do as I tell you, it's not. Otherwise I'll take you up to The Butcher and turn you in. He'd take great pride in dispensing with you."

"What do you want me to do?"

"Upriver, between two right-angle bends, you'll find my pursuit ship. It's a triangular field. Do you know it?"

"You can't get away with this," Blakely began, and then he felt a muzzle prod his ribs. "Yes, I know the place."

"I took off the carburetor and buried it under the nose. And I unfastened the gas line."

"Say, I can't assemble it in the dark!"

"You can and you will. You'll also get ten gallons of gas down at the hangars."

"In these clothes?"

"In those clothes. You'll fill the tank, mount the carburetor, attach the gasoline and scorch for Taiy. Landing there, you'll meet a Russian officer. Tell him to fix up my plane and then lay low yourself and wait for me to get back."

"But I've got my ship here!"

"I know it. But men are down there at the hangar waiting for the bombers to return. You can steal gas, but you could never get your own ship away. Besides, I need a two-seater and that yellow crate of yours is it."

Blakely seemed to choke. "But what are you going to do?"

"That's my business. And don't try anything funny with

that ship because all the machine-gun belts are empty. You'll have to be in Taiy by daylight." He shoved the other away from him. "Get going."

Blakely stood for a long moment trying to see in the dark. Then he wheeled and crept away, heading in the direction of the port. He shied away from a lighted door and went on.

Back in the alley, Wind-Gone-Mad nodded with satisfaction.

CHAPTER FOUR

THE palace of The Butcher was gray in the thickening fog, forbidding and unassailable. An arched tunnel, filled with the stray, slanting beams of hidden lanterns, went in from the street. A soldier as gray and ghostly as the building itself stepped out from a niche and flipped a French bayonet forward.

"Blakely," said Wind-Gone-Mad in the Shen dialect. "To see Hsien-Chung, The Butcher."

Another soldier swung a guttering lantern out of nowhere and splashed its rays into the foreign face. He saw the black helmet and the triangle and bar on the ear tabs. The lantern swung down; the three-cornered bayonet went up, and Wind-Gone-Mad walked on across the slashing paths of other lights.

Ahead, a curved flight of steps led to a higher level, and at the top, on one side of the long corridor, a door swung open. Silhouetted in it was the bulk of a young Chinese officer whose shoulders glittered with braid.

"You are late," said the officer. "This one has waited half an hour. Hsien-Chung, The Butcher, will be enraged if we waste time on our own talk now."

Alert to the import, Wind-Gone-Mad shrugged. "A little time will neither make nor break the empire."

"Then come inside where the walls have no ears." The Chinese stepped aside. "You speak strangely tonight."

Quivering with tension within, but calm without, Wind-Gone-Mad went in and sat down, his back to the light. "The fog."

"But why do you cover your eyes with yellow glass?"

"They are sore with watching for the bombers."

Apparently satisfied, the Chinese seated himself and cleared his throat preliminary to plunging into the business at hand.

"When," he asked, "will the buzzing hornets arrive?"

"The news is delayed," Feng-Feng replied, watchfully.

"It cannot be delayed for long. As soon as Shan Province falls to The Butcher, we can strike with the tide of drunken victory aiding us. After that, we can hurl our forces forward independent of The Butcher's whims."

"It will not be delayed," Wind-Gone-Mad assured him. "Even yourself will be greatly surprised by the speed of the action."

"Wait," muttered the Chinese. "There is something strange about you. There is—" His dark eyes bored deep into the glinting goggles. His long hands clutched the arms of his chair. Abruptly he whirled on a bell rope and stretched out an arm to pull it.

Behind the Chinese there were no sounds to lend haste to the movement. The instant the flash of suspicion appeared on the officer's face, Wind-Gone-Mad had acted. His hand blurred into his topcoat and came out with his gun. In the same movement he threw it spinning across the room. Dully, it smashed flat against the officer's skull.

Wind-Gone-Mad caught the weapon almost before it reached the floor. He watched the Chinese sag down like an empty sack, and then bent swiftly over the body. He hid the officer behind the desk, pulled down the silken panels from the wall, and completed a swift and workmanlike job of binding and gagging the traitor in The Butcher's camp.

He knew what had made him strange. In his anxiety to discover what might lay between this officer and Blakely, he had incautiously spoken the Shen dialect entirely too well. Where Blakely had groped for words and tones, Wind-Gone-Mad had voiced them accurately.

Wind-Gone-Mad turned down the lamp and softly opened the door. The passage was brooding and empty, grimed with age, as harsh and relentless as The Butcher himself.

Wind-Gone-Mad had no illusions about the penalty which would be his, should he be caught in The Butcher's palace. They would impale him on spikes and whip him with shredded bamboo strips which were incredibly sharp. They would make his dying long.

But he thought of Taiy and Cheng-Wang and all that they represented. A kind government over a contented people, exemplary of the China Wind-Gone-Mad was trying to bring about. He remembered Chapei after aerial bombings, saw again the mangled dead in the streets. If he wished to spare Shan Province the horrors attendant to The Butcher's occupation, he would have to act tonight.

The great black door which led to The Butcher lay ahead. On this side there might be some security, but on the other, if he were unmasked, lay exquisite torture.

Wind-Gone-Mad threw back the door and strode in.

Hsien-Chung, The Butcher, crouched behind his desk, his twisted shoulders hunched over a telegram. At the creak of the door, he shot his cruel eyes up over the rim of the yellow sheet, the orbs almost matching the paper. His face was a flat, ill-sculptured blob of putty, blackened by shadow.

"Blakely," he muttered, "you come in time. You have charges to answer."

Wind-Gone-Mad studied The Butcher's face, and in that instant mapped out his campaign. He knew how The Butcher would react, for The Butcher was a type, suffering from severe mental derangement, beleaguered day and night by delusions of persecution, killing because he had to kill to satisfy the cravings of his twisted and inflamed mind.

If he could play upon The Butcher's suspicions, he could guide the rage of the man into profitable channels. But the slightest misstep would call down a legion of guards and, for Wind-Gone-Mad, history would cease.

The Butcher's snarling, guttural tones rasped on. "The bombers did not bomb Taiy. They turned and fled like the yellow curs they are. Here I have a telegram from the front, advising me that it is true."

Wind-Gone-Mad advanced and laid his hands on The Butcher's desk. "Such were the tidings I brought, but my news is greater. You are being betrayed, Hsien-Chung."

The Butcher's eyes flamed coldly. His hands crushed the

telegram. "You tell me what I already know; for once you do not lie with the twisted tongue of a foreign devil. The renegade Feng-Feng is behind this.

"But tomorrow," hissed The Butcher, "all that will be evened. The bombers will return to Taiy. They will smash the city into the bowels of the earth. They will mangle the people in the streets. I will mount the body of Cheng-Wang upon spears and carry him through the town to show them who is their overlord. They will know the fury of my wrath.

"Today is only a delay. They have but postponed their fate. But the delay will be paid for." The Butcher rubbed his hands together. "The renegade called Feng-Feng will be crushed, put aside forever. If I but had him now, there would be sport in the dungeons tonight."

"Wait," replied Wind-Gone-Mad. "You can do none of this if you are surrounded by traitors."

"Traitors?" rasped The Butcher.

"Even the pilots are against you. They think you nothing more than a weak fool."

The Butcher's face was suddenly livid. He raised his hand as if to strike. But the man he thought was Blakely did not flinch.

"They are arriving now," continued Wind-Gone-Mad. "Do you hear the roar of their engines in the distance?"

The Butcher listened, his eyes slitted. "They say I am a weak fool?" He laughed silently. "A weak fool! I will show them! I will kill some of them!"

"That is a wise course," nodded Wind-Gone-Mad. "A wise solution."

Wind-Gone-Mad realized, now, that the removal of The Butcher would not straighten matters out. With that officer plotting against him, the absence of The Butcher would do but little to save Taiy.

However, The Butcher was a menace. He would have to be gotten out of the way. The Butcher's insane lust had been imparted to his officers, and the war would go on. But if he could take The Butcher away and then stop the bombers before they accomplished their gruesome work, Wind-Gone-Mad's campaign would succeed.

"In order that they do not know, your excellency, I have a small machine gun at the hangar. Knowing your marksmanship—"

"Yes," hissed The Butcher, quivering with eagerness.

"You can take it and kill them with your own hands. Then we will get other pilots. That will teach all traitors to beware."

"It will teach all traitors— Good! I will kill them for their treachery. We will take a guard—"

Wind-Gone-Mad's voice was almost a whisper. "But some of your guards are against you. They might turn on you in the darkness."

"Ah! I knew they were. Long have I felt it. Come, we will take a car and go. You are sure your machine gun is ready?"

"I am sure," said Wind-Gone-Mad, and followed The Butcher through a panel and into a passage which led out of the palace.

His luck, so far, had held. But he knew that he had solved nothing. If The Butcher meant nothing to the young officer as a hostage, then Taiy would be bombed and laid in ruins.

All the terrible consequences of invasion would not be stayed. But with The Butcher out of the picture, Wind-Gone-Mad would feel a little more at ease. He could at least reason with a sane man.

While Hsien-Chung, The Butcher, stood waiting in the darkness, Wind-Gone-Mad slipped into the private garage, waved away an inquiring chauffeur and drove out in a small foreign car. He was thankful that Blakely had made himself so well-known around the palace.

The Butcher eased, catlike, into the front seat to sit in a crouch, glowering through the windshield with slitted eyes which held raw lust.

"You are sure you have the machine gun?" hissed the provincial governor above the purr of the motor. "How do I know that you do not lie?"

"Have I ever lied to you before?"

They rode into fog which increased steadily as they neared the river. Wind-Gone-Mad drove circuitously, avoiding the main cobblestone thoroughfare to the airport. He knew that the bomber pilots and mechanics would be cleared away by this time, anxious to make their appearance before The Butcher, probably understanding that the orders had been a ruse, probably shaking with fear before The Butcher's ever-to-be-expected wrath.

Coasting with silent motor for the last hundred yards, they neared the squatty hangar. Wind-Gone-Mad braked and listened. All was still save for the burbling of the river not far away. Only a watchman's light showed through the rough window of the spreading structure.

Unwitting, in his single-track greed for killing, The Butcher made an animal-like noise in his thick throat. "Where is the machine gun?"

"Here," said Wind-Gone-Mad, and stabbed The Butcher's ribs with his automatic. "One sound and I'll blow you apart."

A vague shape in the mist, The Butcher's head jerked back with surprise. The hangar light caught sharply at the burning rectangles which were his eyes. A sharp rustle of silk warned Feng-Feng of a sudden action. Light danced on the blade of a knife.

Fighting from under a wheel was not simple. Wind-Gone-Mad twisted valiantly about, grasped the upheld wrist, and gave it a savage wrench. The knife tinkled bell-like on the running board. The Butcher's teeth gleamed and, divining the attempt to yell before it was actually made, Feng-Feng released the wrist and slapped a hand over The Butcher's mouth. The sharp fangs sent a sickening wave of pain up Wind-Gone-Mad's arm, but he held the palm tight.

The Butcher gurgled and jerked away, fumbling for another weapon. Steel shimmered for an instant in his hand. But the speed of the move was bettered. Before The Butcher could release his safety catch, even while it still clicked, Wind-Gone-Mad swept down with the butt of his own gun.

Hsien-Chung, The Butcher, writhed, fumbled, dropped his own weapon and then fell limply back. He gazed emptily at the roof of the car, his brutish jaw quite slack.

There was little time to spare; but for an instant, Wind-Gone-Mad felt tempted to take one of the great bombers back to Taiy. Then he realized that their tanks would be empty, and that the other bombers would not be far behind. And then, too, the bomb load still nestled dangerously under the ships. No, he would take the yellow plane of Blakely's. After all, he had said that he would. He would have to be in Taiy before daylight.

He darted into the back door of the hangar and glanced around. Two soldiers stood out in the great maw, facing the three air giants which had not yet been put to bed, so great had been the haste of the crews to explain. Fog drifted in thin wisps across the bows of the ships and between the struts of the two-seater observation plane which Blakely used.

Wind-Gone-Mad strode boldly toward the two soldiers and when they turned, startled at the sound of footsteps, he roared at them, "Where are the others? Where are the pilots?"

"Have you not heard?" jabbered one, excitedly. "He they call Feng-Feng was here. We saw him with our own eyes. He was like a great devil. His teeth were long and dripping blood. His hands were claws like those of an eagle. He was here for a moment but with a spire of flame he was gone."

"The pilots have gone for the others and for Hsien-Chung, The Butcher. We will catch this devil tonight." The other soldier stopped and they all heard the far-off throb of an engine.

Wind-Gone-Mad knew that it was Blakely getting away. He could tell by the uncertain note that the engine was getting warm.

"Go after him!" bawled Feng-Feng gesticulating wildly. "Get him before he is gone into the sky."

The first soldier was startled by the thought. "But the others will be here in an instant. We cannot desert—"

"Go!" bellowed Wind-Gone-Mad. "The others will come to help you. A reward is yours if you stop him!"

The two licked their lips, glanced at one another, and then as though afraid to expose their fear, they charged out into the fog toward the rapidly growing sound. Blakely, Feng-Feng knew, was safely off the ground.

Darting back to the car, Wind-Gone-Mad dragged The Butcher into the hangar and threw him bodily into the front cockpit of the yellow plane. With a roll of brass safety wire he tied him there. With a wad of cotton waste he made certain that the Chinese could utter no sound of warning.

That done, Wind-Gone-Mad headed for the three bombers, a wrench and a hammer in his hand. A glance up the hill showed him that the palace was bathed in many lights. They were searching for The Butcher, and in a matter of minutes they would avalanche down on the airport.

He worked fast and expertly, standing on an ascending ladder to reach the bomb racks. But before he had completed a fraction of the work, he knew that it was impossible. There were too many bombs and too much plane. The wing reared above him like an auditorium roof and the fuselage stretched out like the dry-docked hull of a battleship. He did not dare show a light.

He was forced to content himself with the ton demolition bombs of which each plane had two. He was thankful to note that Demming Aircraft had palmed off wartime shells on The Butcher. It was a simple matter to unscrew the detonators, thereby rendering the sleek hulls of destruction useless. The high explosive would not explode without its percussion cap.

At the hangar side he piled the six detonators and then returned to the ships. For a moment he stood regarding the single high wing of the first and then, tightening his hold on hammer and wrench, he climbed aboard, feeling like a steeplejack.

Up on the hillside the lights were going out. But a white blur in the streets warned that cars were rolling. In an instant, the soldiers and pilots would arrive.

Wind-Gone-Mad climbed down off the third ship and ran to the yellow plane. He threw the switch, pulled the club and held his breath until the engine came alive.

When he climbed in, juggling a dark object gingerly, he saw The Butcher squirm. Wind-Gone-Mad smiled and tested the throttle. The edge of the field was white with fog-blurred lights. One of the soldiers he had sent away loped into view, startled at the engine's roar. Hoarsely, the Chinese screamed.

The two-seater's engine tried valiantly to take her gas. It spluttered, caught, spluttered again. It was cold and raw fluid clogged in the cylinders. Sluggishly, the yellow plane rolled forward.

Someone had reached the floodlight switch, and Wind-Gone-Mad commented to himself that The Butcher had certainly bought the works. In spite of the curling gray mist, it was as though the sun had risen.

The soldier saw The Butcher and bellowed again. A rifle flashed; its bullet went wild. Picking up speed with heart-breaking slowness, the ship trundled past the bombers, under the spreading wings. Someone had unleashed a machine gun, utterly disregarding the intelligence that Hsien-Chung,

The Butcher, was in the yellow plane. Holes marched down a wing and then came back, making a double path.

Abruptly, the motor ceased to cough and its bellow swelled out into an even, strident roar. Air fled over the cowl and the wheels lightened on the fleeing ground. Juggling the stick, Wind-Gone-Mad bounced the ship, figuratively wishing it into the air.

Holding level for a moment, picking up air speed, he banked vertically and came howling back. He held one of the detonators in his hand, and when he passed the machine gun below he hurled the object down. Behind him there was a dull red flash. The machine gun stopped. The floodlights were gone.

Wind-Gone-Mad looked at the head in the front cockpit and then back at the panel. He did not worry about how The Butcher was taking it. It would take a great deal of navigation to get the two-seater over the yellow-rusty mountains and back to Taiy.

CHAPTER FIVE

A T eight o'clock, with the morning sun struggling to pierce the gray haze, the tidings that Wind-Gone-Mad had returned with the captive Butcher were suddenly eclipsed by news of far more sinister portent.

A group of men stood on the flat, embrasured top of a tall palace building in Shan, gazing anxiously southeast.

Wind-Gone-Mad, dressed once more in his own outfit and masked by his goggles, stood beside a gun port and scrutinized the plain with a powerful set of binoculars. From time to time he pointed the lenses up over the horizon in search of the bombers.

"You're thorough," Wind-Gone-Mad told Blakely. "Since when did you find it necessary to tie up with an arms company?"

Blakely adjusted his black scarf, his dark eyes sullen, his lean face haggard. "If I want to make a contract with Westchester Arms, that's my business."

"Westchester Arms and how many others?" said Wind-Gone-Mad without taking down the field glasses. "It's a long jump from bombing planes to armored cars."

"You have to have armored cars to hold a bombed position, don't you?" countered Blakely. He glanced uneasily at the two soldiers who stood beside him with bayonets fixed. "You can't hold a man for trying to make a little money, can you?"

"No, you can't. But what makes me a little peeved is that you'd take a jump at being a warlord yourself. It isn't done."

Blakely's eyes narrowed. "Meaning?"

"That you ordered pursuit planes for your own use."

"You're too smart, renegade," mocked Blakely. "I suppose you know that bringing The Butcher here did you no good whatever."

"I know that now. But the sortie was not without its points. You'll grant me that, I hope. The young Chinese general I left on the ground couldn't possibly raise as much dust as The Butcher."

Blakely grunted. "He's sane at least. But you put your neatly booted foot into it when you brought me back here."

"I had to get my own ship home, didn't I? And it wouldn't carry two, would it?" The binoculars swept in another swift arc and then came to rest. "Three dots out there on the plain. How many armored cars have they got?"

"Five," Blakely snapped. "And five is plenty. When the bombers come over and lay their eggs, those motorized forts will sweep in here with all bullets in the fire. There won't be a man or woman alive in this town by noon."

"Including yourself," remarked Wind-Gone-Mad.

Blakely blinked and growled, "You think it's clever, I suppose. Bringing The Butcher and myself back here to be killed by my planes and guns."

"Fitting justice."

Cheng-Wang hobbled out of the doorway and came across the roof holding his thin hands in the crooks of his arms as though cold. His heavily brocaded gown rustled in the silence.

Behind him walked a communications man who dragged a length of telephone line and who carried a field instrument over his shoulder. At a motion from Cheng-Wang he set the golden oak box down beside Wind-Gone-Mad on the stone embrasure.

"Kerensk, the Russian," said Cheng-Wang, "wishes to speak to Feng-Feng from the airport."

For the first time, Wind-Gone-Mad laid down the field glasses. He picked up the shining instrument with a side glance at Blakely.

"Listen," said Kerensk, the Russian. "I have been talking with the general now in command at Sing, using your plane set."

"You told him that any attack would result in the death of The Butcher?"

"Yes," replied Kerensk. "I told him and he remarked that it was good. He remarked that he was glad The Butcher would die. He said that the bombers had already left Sing and that we still had another hour to surrender. He also said that five armored cars and many truckloads of troops had blasted our frontier and were now only waiting for the preparatory aerial attack."

"He is full of information," said Wind-Gone-Mad. "Truly, he is a wise man."

Kerensk chuckled. "Truly, he is. But I was not lacking in data. I most politely informed him that we had masked antiaircraft batteries awaiting the bombing planes and that the worthy pilots had better fly high."

"You have an excellent imagination," replied Wind-Gone-Mad.

"If the fount of wisdom spurts again, give me a buzz." He hung up and turned to Cheng-Wang. "Where are you keeping Hsien-Chung, The Butcher?"

"He is below on the bottom floor inside the door leading to the great courtyard. His blood is ice." Cheng-Wang permitted himself a smile.

"As he has inspired great terror, he now inspires great fear within himself. Let the order be given that his guards are not to shoot should Hsien-Chung, The Butcher, attempt to escape."

Cheng-Wang lifted his sparse white brows and his fingernails clicked. But before he could relay the order, Wind-Gone-Mad was speaking again.

"And now," said Wind-Gone-Mad in a calm voice, "now come the bombers."

A throbbing of great motors steadily swelled in volume and three dots on the horizon steadily increased in size. Twenty-seven tons of death—all but the demolition bombs intact—was ready to spray itself over the city of Taiy.

With each swelling *haroooom-haroooom!* Blakely's eyes grew wider and blacker. He twisted inside his topcoat and shakily passed his hand through his sparse black hair.

"You might at least let me go down below," quavered Blakely, his nerve leaving him. "This will be the first target and this is the most exposed position in the town."

"Stay where you are," snapped Wind-Gone-Mad, field glasses restless, "or I myself will be the first to put a bullet in your back."

"That's better than being blown to atoms!" cried Blakely,

but, nevertheless, he stood in his place and watched the birds of his company's creation grow in appalling size. Wind-Gone-Mad's holster was tied with leather to his thigh and Wind-Gone-Mad could draw with unbelievable speed. The soldiers showed no signs of terror, no matter what they felt. Their bayonets were ready and their faith in the man called Feng-Feng was supreme.

"Cheng-Wang!" rapped Wind-Gone-Mad. "Give the order that no batteries are to fire at those planes."

Cheng-Wang was shaken. There were twenty 75s within the city and upon them Cheng-Wang had placed a great deal of hope. "No firing? But we shall be obliterated, hammered to bits!"

"Give the order," replied Wind-Gone-Mad, coolly, and Cheng-Wang turned to obey.

Out of the yellow expanse of plain, five armored cars increased in detail until they were not more than five hundred yards from the outer edge of the town. There they paused, cruising back and forth, keeping out of the bombing radius, waiting for their turn to mop up the gashed rubble the bombers would leave.

Ten thousand feet in the air, the bombers had arrived over the town.

"Too high for accuracy," Wind-Gone-Mad informed Cheng-Wang. "They will drop their ton demolition bombs and then dive lower to finish up with their smaller missiles."

Only half-reassured, Cheng-Wang stood with folded arms, slightly hunched, looking up with the manner of the hypnotized.

Blakely was pressing himself close against the wall, crouching low, his teeth chattering like a snare drum.

Coolly, Wind-Gone-Mad waited for black shapes to drop away from the great bellies. He picked up the phone and received a connection with the batteries of 75s.

"Wait," said Wind-Gone-Mad, "until the great birds drop down low in a dive. They will come from the windward. Concentrate all cannon with that in mind and wait for my order." Tense replies rattled back to him.

Slowly at first, then picking up speed and straightening out, the ton demolition bombs came away from the great ships. It was all too apparent that they would strike either the courtyard or the roof. Blakely was frozen with fear.

Abruptly, from below, there came a babble of sound. A roar of shouting men. Wind-Gone-Mad looked over the edge of the embrasure in time to see Hsien-Chung, The Butcher, hurl himself out into the open. Obeying their order not to shoot, afraid to expose themselves, soldiers huddled back in the doorway.

"Stop!" shrieked The Butcher, shaking futile fists at the sky. "The Butcher is here. Hold your bombs on the pain of death!" Terror contorted the bestial face. Fear that had gone beyond all control. The Butcher's twisted mind had snapped.

Down came the ton demolitions, picking up speed, spinning, beyond the halting hand of all men. The first crunched into a wall; the second crumpled against the cobblestones; the rest struck almost simultaneously.

But without their detonators, they did not explode. They

Stories
from the
Golden Age
by L. Ron Hubbard

Join the Stories from the Golden Age Book Club Today!

Yes! Sign me up for the Book Club (*check one of the following*) and each month I will receive:

○ One paperback book at $9.95 a month.

○ Or, one unabridged audiobook CD at the cost of $9.95 a month.

Book Club members get FREE SHIPPING **and handling** (applies to US residents only).

Name   (please print)

If under 18, signature of guardian

Address

City   State   ZIP   Telephone

E-mail

You may sign up by doing any of the following:

1. To pay by credit card go online at www.goldenagestories.com

2. Call toll-free 1-877-842-5299 or fax this card in to 1-323-466-7817

3. Send in this card with a check for the first month
   payable to Galaxy Press

To get a FREE Stories from
the Golden Age catalog check here ○
and mail or fax in this card.

Thank you!

Subscribe today!
And get a FREE gift.

For details, go to www.goldenagestories.com.

For an up-to-date listing of available titles visit www.goldenagestories.com

Stories
from the
Golden Age
by
L. Ron Hubbard

BUSINESS REPLY MAIL

FIRST-CLASS MAIL   PERMIT NO. 75738   LOS ANGELES CA

POSTAGE WILL BE PAID BY ADDRESSEE

GOLDEN AGE BOOK CLUB
GALAXY PRESS
7051 HOLLYWOOD BLVD
LOS ANGELES CA 90028-9771

chipped out a fine spray of mortar and stone, telescoped their
thin shells, rolled a few feet and spilled out their TNT into
harmless piles.

In the courtyard, The Butcher had fallen on his face. He lay
inert, unmarked as far as Wind-Gone-Mad could ascertain
from above. The soldiers in the doorway showed no wish to
drag him back into shelter.

Wind-Gone-Mad turned to the white-faced, shaking
Blakely. "Rotten bombs you sold them." Knowing Blakely
to be incapable of answering at that moment, he picked up
the field phone and called Kerensk. "Dud bombs," he said.
"What are they radioing to one another?"

"They're going downward," the Russian crackled. "They're
coming lower to drop their smaller bombs, and there will be
plenty of those."

Wind-Gone-Mad hung up and waited. He lifted the
receiver and contacted the batteries of 75s. "Hold your fire
until I give the word."

In the space of five minutes, the three bombers had circled
around to the southeast and were angling down, full power,
toward Taiy. Wind-Gone-Mad smiled tightly and waited,
the word "Fire!" forming on his lips. He knew that the 75s
could not hope to hit the bombers, but they could at least
scare the pilots. That was what Wind-Gone-Mad required.
Cheng-Wang crouched tensely, his eyes traveling jerkily
between his savior and the planes.

Coming at a speed of nearly two hundred miles an hour,
wings vibrating in their dive, the size of the bombers seemed

to double with every second. Death crouched close beneath their great bellies, waiting to be tripped. Three thousand feet up they were not yet over the armored cars.

"Fire!" bellowed Wind-Gone-Mad into the phone.

Almost before the word was out of his tight mouth, a screaming barrage of shrapnel burst in a great cloud before the planes. Though no hit was registered, the noses of the giants jutted suddenly up, jerked by surprised hands.

Cheng-Wang gasped. And well he might. Where ships had been an instant before there was now a fluttering mass of wings out of which three fuselages hurtled down. Almost before a clock could tick, parachutes bellied out over the stripped hulls.

"The wings came off!" gasped Blakely.

"Sure," replied Wind-Gone-Mad. "Fine planes your outfit makes."

The remark was drowned by the roar of the exploding bomb loads. The plain was suddenly a volcano crater which boiled out struts and wheels. Two armored cars lay on their sides; the remaining three were scuttling erratically south.

Wind-Gone-Mad saw soldiers pick up The Butcher and bring him into the palace. Turning to the soldiers and Cheng-Wang he motioned that they go below, taking Blakely with them. When they had gone, Wind-Gone-Mad turned again to the phone.

"Kerensk?" And when the Russian had answered: "The red paint and the red dragon on my plane will rub off nicely. Be sure that the Amalgamated Aeronautical shield is prominent on the black sides. Gas her up and wait for me there."

In the reception room of the palace, Hsien-Chung, The Butcher, or rather his earthly remains, was laid upon a blackwood couch. Blakely stood beside him, feeling for the pulse, his eyes sullen.

"He's dead," said Blakely, his voice weary.

"Frightened to death, I suppose," said Wind-Gone-Mad. "I thought, Blakely, that you were not good at sales talks. Your speeches about the death-dealing qualities of those bombers and bombs proved too much for him. He was about ready to crack, anyway. In psychiatry, they would call him schizophrenic."

Blakely's brooding eyes swept over Wind-Gone-Mad. "Whatever he was, he's dead. You've ruined a lot of good business for me, pirate. And one of these days I'll see to it that your head hangs high. You have mighty hands against you."

Wind-Gone-Mad smiled. "And mighty ones pushing me along. It's only fair to you, Blakely, to tell you that your planes were not faulty. I stripped off their jury struts last night. And I loosened the pins which held the others. In a power dive, the whole wing gave way."

Blakely's face darkened, but he said nothing.

Wind-Gone-Mad turned to Cheng-Wang. "A young Chinese is in charge of Shen Province now. He will doubtless cancel his order for more planes. The pilots who parachuted to safety can be sold back to him for the price of peace. He dares not let either them or Blakely down." He pulled a blank out of his shirt and handed it to Cheng-Wang.

"This is an order for ten pursuit ships," continued

Wind-Gone-Mad. "They will be delivered and pilots will be sent. This is an additional guarantee of peace. Please sign."

Cheng-Wang signed with three stabs of his paint brush, his old face peaceful, his hands unshaking. "And Jim Dahlgren, your friend, will deliver them."

"Sure he will," muttered Blakely. "And then this pirate can garner his pay."

Wind-Gone-Mad strode to the door which a soldier swung open before him. He turned back for a moment, his goggles flashing. "Let no man go away from this palace before dark, that I may get away. That is all that I require."

Boot heels drumming on the stone, he went outside. The black doors swung softly shut behind him.

A week later, Jim Dahlgren, of Amalgamated Aeronautical Co., sat at the conference table with the foreign officers who were the Chinese powers that be. His gray eyes were at ease, his blond hair unruffled. His face showed that he had but lately flown, for the goggle marks were white against the tan of his lower jaw.

The C-in-C of the USN continued his monologue. "In spite of the obvious manner in which this affair was conducted, I am, nevertheless, grateful for its successful conclusion. We might object, Dahlgren, to the fact that you profit by the affair, but after all, it was your connection which cleared the matter up.

"However, if you see this man called Wind-Gone-Mad again, inform him for us that he cannot act the pirate for long and that capture by any of five nations will mean immediate trial and possible execution. The man's efforts are, after all, beyond the pale of law." He leaned back, signifying that the matter was closed.

The Italian officer smiled companionably at Dahlgren. As the meeting was at a close, he felt that a few personal remarks would not be out of order. "You have been flying, Mr. Dahlgren?"

"Canton," said the Amalgamated salesman. "A little business."

"It must have been somewhat interesting." His smile turned into an insinuating grin. "The little lady must have bitten you, judging from the teeth marks on your hand."

Jim Dahlgren did not lose his composure. He merely smiled and glanced down at the fang prints The Butcher had left upon him.

"Oh, that?" replied Jim Dahlgren, the respectable plane salesman. "A dog did that. A mongrel dog that wouldn't listen to reason."

Тан

TAH

LITTLE Tah walked back and forth before General Chang's tent and watched his square footprints following themselves in the thick dust. He had shined his shoes that morning with the aid of some goose grease, but now there remained only the dull sheen of oil-accumulated dirt. The gun on little Tah's shoulder had grown very heavy during the last three hours, but a soldier never complained, even at death.

The army of Chang had been camped in the center of this yellow plain for two weeks, enough time to thwart the efforts of foragers, and to exhaust the patience of the few scattered farmers whose fields had been trammeled by five thousand men a week before the harvest. But the sick were becoming strong again, and the morale had risen through many nights of sitting around flickering campfires with nothing more in mind than a long sleep in a warm bed under a clear sky. Little Tah had noticed the difference, and had confided in Trivenak, the sublieutenant of the boy's company, while the White Russian had wound a bandage around the little bruised hand of his twelve-year-old soldier.

"You'll make a general some day, Tah," still rang in the ears of the boy. He looked down at his cotton-padded gray uniform and wondered how gold braid must feel when it graced a silken tunic. He dared peek into the tent of the commander as he passed by, and started a little when he saw the general sprawled on his cot, his mouth open in heavy sleep. Did one suddenly look like that when one became a general? Tah liked to think of generals in terms of Trivenak, who was straight and carried his mouth with just the right amount of authority. But if Trivenak thought that Tah would make a general some day, Tah would try.

The footprints became overlaid with others. The dust eddied about the square shoes, and the twelve-year-old Chinese soldier's mind turned to other more important things. Tsing had made a new top he wanted Tah to see. It must be a glorious top, for Tsing had made it, and though Tsing was a year younger than the sentry, he possessed a knack of making beautiful things of wood. When this tour of duty was ended, he would search out Wung and the two of them would find Tsing and ask him to spin the top for them. Wung could draw pictures with charcoal on stone. Little Tah liked pictures, especially pictures of gardens with big birds singing on top of the shrines and waterfalls bubbling away. He wished he could draw pictures. He sighed as he made his five-hundredth about-face at the end of the tent, but brightened when he thought of his new marksmanship record which had brought him this heavy gun. Ninety-five out of a possible one hundred. But still he wished he could draw pictures like those of the eleven-year-old Wung, or make tops like Tsing could.

A company of infantry marched down the gouged road throwing geysers of dust into the hot air, their rifles askew and their bandoliers clanking against their buttons. The company halted while the captain hurried over to the general's tent. Little Tah stood at attention, his rifle just the height of his pillbox cap, and demanded the officer's business.

"Tell your General Chang that I come from Harbin with important news. Hurry!"

Tah stalked into the tent, his rifle dragging, and shook the general by the shoulder. Chang sat up stifling a yawn to pull his sword belt around his fat stomach which bulged when the buckle was fastened. The officer entered and Tah retired to resume his pacings back and forth. If he hadn't been thinking so hard about his two friends, he might have heard an exciting conversation. At the six-hundredth about-face, a grizzled Manchurian relieved Tah of his post.

Tah wiped some of the dust from his shoes, the gun grease from his gray-clad shoulder, and went in search of Wung, whom he found seated on the pointer's ledge of a worn-out seventy-five.

"Seen Tsing?" Tah leaned his rifle against a wheel of the cannon, and seated himself on the trace.

"No, Tsing on range with company." Wung's deep brown eyes followed the tracing his stick made in the sand.

"Seen top?" A slight frown passed over Tah's face as he gazed at his friend.

"No. You?" Wung's expression was impassive.

"Heart bad?" Tah moved closer to his friend and put an arm across the dejected shoulders.

"Think too much today. Remember gracious father."

"Sorry. Can do something?"

"No. Chang shoot soldier who run. Good soldier do not

run. Wung good soldier like Tah and Tsing. They of good heart."

"Tah like to see his gracious father, too, but father sell Tah to Chang. What can Tah do?"

"Does Tah like to be soldier way down in heart?"

"Hush. There bugle blow!"

The staccato notes of assembly rang out across the plain. Soldiers were running from everywhere toward their companies.

Tah plucked at Wung's sleeve. "Come. Maybe we go again."

Trivenak was bawling orders to a ragged line of soldiers who wrestled with equipment, their guns braced between their knees. Trivenak aided some of them with their packs, and then with a final glance at the now-straight line, turned the company over to the approaching captain.

A bugle blew again, and five thousand men moved out onto the dust-choked road toward the north. Little Tah's heavy rifle felt like fire on his shoulder. Each time he stepped, the rough sling seemed to sear the young flesh beneath the gray tunic.

"E! UR! SEN! SHU! E! UR! SEN! SHU! HEP! UR! SEN! SHU!"

Boots rose and fell, almost invisible through the cloud which increased at each step to crowd deeper into little Tah's throat. Wung, on Tah's left, was walking with lowered head, and in spite of his own misery, Tah felt a quick pang of sympathy as he saw a tear roll down his comrade's face. Tsing, on Tah's right, gave his friend a long sidewise look and then threw his shoulders back to gaze up at the cap ahead of him. He was a soldier!

There were no ten-minute rest periods today, and at every

count, Tah thought he heard the tempo of the march quicken. The rifle grew to be a dull ache as the straps of his pack gnawed at his narrow shoulders. Tah thought for a moment of his home in Mukden where he had attended school until a year ago. There one did not choke on dust and have packs beat down one's shoulders. He remembered how pleasant the room had been with its screens and low tables, its cushions and its kindly master.

"E! UR! SEN! SHU! HEP! UR! SEN! SHU!"

Tah remembered how he had wept when the master had once beat him across the back with a willow switch for upsetting ink. The pack was slipping a little and threw the boy's stride off. He glanced at a file closer, barely discernible through the yellow cloud, and hastily shifted his rifle to his left shoulder. Would they never give the command for route step? Or were they too hurried to delay the five thousand with stragglers? Tah remembered that he would make a general some day and felt a little better.

"E! UR! SEN! SHU!"

Did they have to count everything? Tah wondered if his family ever thought about him. Probably not, with ten mouths to feed. Was mother still well? His lips were cracking with the dryness of the air. The sore on the right side was getting bad. Those boots looked odd, going up and down, up and down. Wung was still crying. He had only run away from home three months ago. Tah remembered how *he* had cried when he had first come out to this eternal war. That bulge in Tsing's pocket must be his top. Tah wished he had had a chance to see it spin. Tsing had said it really was wonderful.

"E! UR! SEN! SHU!"

It must be getting late. The dust was not sparkling anymore. There was a temple in Mukden whose bells must be ringing now. Tah thought of the countless times he had walked up the high steps into the garden which lay beyond the second wall. The birds always seemed to whistle at him when he came, and the goldfish seemed to swim faster when he looked at them. It was quiet in that garden.

"HEP! UR! SEN! SHU! E! UR!—"

And the yellow-robed monk had offered to teach him all the songs, that he, too, might wear the robe when he grew older. It was dark now, and Tah couldn't see the boots anymore. He felt as if he were alone in spite of the steady beat of shoes on the road. Tah could feel the dust settling heavily on his face and uniform. The rifle was hurting his left shoulder. Breaking his pace a moment, Tah loosened the sling and slung the weapon across the top of his pack. A hasty adjustment of buckles brought the weight above his shoulder blades. That was better. Monks didn't have to carry packs at all. They sat on little yellow cushions and chanted while bull fiddles droned somewhere in the darkness of the temple. Robes weren't as heavy as packs, and monks didn't have to listen to

"HEP! UR! SEN! SHU!"

The road was growing rougher. Tah realized that his feet were becoming blistered. They would stop before long and Tah would place some goose grease around his heels so that they wouldn't swell. Last month he had been unable to remove his shoes after an all-night march. The sharper stones bruised the boy's instep.

At midnight a halt was called that the weary men might shed their packs for a moment's rest. Tah set his gear in the road between Tsing's and Wung's, pausing for a moment before he squatted on his heels, to look at the stars.

Wung coughed at his elbow. "Tired!"

"No. Stars pretty, Wung."

"Rifle hurts." Wung sat down on his pack and fell forward sound asleep. Tsing had cast himself full length in the dirt to bury his head in his arms.

Tah thought for a moment about his heels, but as he knelt to dig into his duffle, he, too, collapsed to sprawl beside his friends, his face turned to the stars.

Trivenak stopped for a moment to look down at the young face and sighed. The skin was still soft like a baby's, but the wrinkles around the eyes belied Tah's twelve years. Trivenak started to kneel beside the boy, but squared his shoulders and strode on down the line to check the numbers of his company.

Although they had been halted fifteen minutes, Tah felt that it had been less than one. His shoulders were stiff from the momentary relaxation and his boots felt ugly and cold. He helped Wung adjust his pack and fixed Tsing's rifle so that it could be carried by the sling, and had barely shouldered his own burden when the five thousand began to move.

"E! UR! SEN! SHU! HEP! UR! SEN! SHU!"

The dust was writhing up into the air again to blot out the stars. Tah felt his heels trod upon and sluggishly caught the step. He wished he had remembered the goose grease. His heels felt worse for the halt. How he hated to start out again with cold boots! It would have been better to have kept right on marching. He was glad it was too dark to see the feet ahead of him.

At five o'clock the long column began to stop at intervals, and Tah surmised that the companies up front were being dispersed. After slouching up the road ten yards at a time, Tah's weary company at last came to a trench. It was long, and seemingly without end to its black length. For the first time, Tah became conscious of a dull booming and a high crackle which had long been in his ears. He had heard it months before and knew that the rumble was made by large guns, and that the crackle was that of rifles and machine guns.

The east was gradually turning gray, and the cold morning air bit into Tah as he stood at the top of a parapet waiting for Trivenak to give an order. The White Russian shouted, and the men tumbled into the trench to sink as one man on the fire step where they huddled together in sleep. Tah was too tired to rest. He lay close to his friends with his eyes on the graying sky. Wung was whimpering softly, though he slept.

Nine o'clock found the five thousand waiting at attention in the trenches. The rumble had grown louder, and far down the line, Tah could hear the mad clatter of machine guns. Smoke had begun to roll across the yellow plain before them. There were some hills two or three miles away which Tah liked. There were green spots there. Tah wondered how it would feel to sprawl at full length in tall, damp grass. He moved and a cloud of dust rolled from him.

Some little figures in gray were running across the plains toward them. Tah tried to count them, but his eyes smarted. The figures were coming nearer. Trivenak stood up on the parapet and watched them through a pair of field glasses. The crackling was growing louder now, and above his head, Tah could hear the vicious twang of bullets. He knew that they were rifle bullets. He looked at the figures again, and saw some of them kneel, get up, run closer, throw themselves on the ground, get up again. There were more than he had supposed. Dully he wondered who they were and why they were kneeling.

Trivenak turned toward the far end of the line, and then waved his hand. "Ready on the firing line!" he bellowed. "Load!"

Tah's deep brown eyes sprung wide for a moment and then he bent to pick a clip out of his bandolier. He felt the cartridges slither out of the clip and into the breech. He slammed home the bolt and set his sights for a thousand yards.

Trivenak looked out across the plains for a moment and then threw down his arm. "Fire!"

Tah stood on his pack and thrust his rifle toward the gray figures which grew closer every second. His finger pressed the trigger. The recoil almost knocked him away from the parapet. He slammed another shell into the barrel. He tried to aim but the gun shook. He pressed the trigger, loaded, pressed the trigger. The gray figures were close to the trench. Out of the corner of his eye, Tah saw Trivenak spin around and crumple into the trench, half his face gone. Tah's rifle grew hot. He couldn't see the sights. Clip after clip he tore off the bandolier and rattled into the magazine. Tears were blinding him. The acrid taste of smokeless powder was in his mouth.

Load and fire! Load and fire! On his right, Wung cried out. Tah turned to see the child clutch at the sandbags, and then hurtle onto the dusty floor. Load and fire! The gray figures were almost to the trench. Tah could see them falling here and there, but the tide swept on over the bodies. Load and fire! Tsing snatched at his arm, tried to say something. Tsing coughed and thick blood drooled out of his mouth. Tsing's face fell forward against the wall. Tah heard the death rattle. Load and fire! A huge face leered in back of a bayonet. The bayonet was coming nearer, nearer. The bayonet was long, a thousand miles long. There was red on the end. Tah felt the icy, burning steel rasp against the bones in his chest. The leering face was tugging at the rifle. Tah's body surged back and forth as the face tried to free the bayonet. There was a sheet of flame as the face pulled the trigger. The rifle came free. Burning powder was eating at Tah's little face. He fell back into the trench across the body of Wung. There was the sky above, all blue and clean. Tah retched. His breast was on fire. Huge waves of rugged pain clutched at his heart. He felt dust beneath his blackened fingers. His little hand plucked at it weakly. There was the sky above, all blue and clean. He couldn't think. A top spun before his eyes. Tsing's top. He would wake up in a minute and go to school. The pain tore at his heart. There was a black cloud up there now. He tried to move. Dust was everywhere. Black dust settling across his eyes. His heart didn't hurt now. The dust settled more thickly. He felt himself falling, falling, falling. Black dust. Falling, falling. Everything would be all right in a moment.

YELLOW LOOT

YELLOW LOOT

A N ugly laugh behind them made all six white men jerk their heads towards the entrance of the tomblike room. A Chinese voice remarked, "It was kind of you to lead us here, for we have been trying unsuccessfully for years to discover the hiding place of that amber."

A gray-uniformed Chinaman strode into the room, an ugly automatic in his dirty right hand. His left hand motioned in the direction of the jewelry one of the men had just brought out from the aged wall safe.

"Please put up your hands," he requested.

Of the six white men, five immediately reached for the moist, dark ceiling, but the sixth did not move. Brad Williams was not the type who easily gives up.

It was only out of relationship to Jeremiah Williams, leader of the archaeological expedition, that Brad Williams had consented at all to accompany these seemingly helpless scientists to the Chang tombs north of Peking. Brad had told the others of the dangers they were running, but they had laughed at him, jeered at him as being young and imaginative—and now here was the proof.

Too late, the five scientists realized that the ugly rumors which came down from the Western Hills were more than rumors.

Brad dared not guess at the fate which menaced them. Certainly it would seem that the fortune in century-old amber which they had just unearthed would be enough to occupy the mind of the bandit who stood before them, but again—one never knew just what might occur.

And Brad felt responsible for these white men. His uncle, Jeremiah Williams, seemed frail and weak in spite of the acidity of his face and temper.

Brad stared at the gray-clad officer and his eyes became as chill as blue ice. As soon as the Chinaman shifted to look at the amber, Brad tensed himself. Then, like a panther, he leaped. The automatic spat flame, but Brad found the other's throat in his two hands.

The Chinaman swayed back, tried to bring up the pistol, but Brad was on top of him, hitting him with hammerlike fists. The five scientists stood about, their hands still on high, and goggled at the sight, while their flashlights pointed at the wet ceiling of the underground pagoda room.

The Chinaman brought the automatic down, narrowly missing Brad's head, then grunted as the American sank savage fists into his chest and stomach. The man suddenly crumpled and dropped to the floor, his gun clattering on the stone.

Brad stared down for an instant, then he snatched up the pistol and whirled about. "Pick up that amber! Let's get out of here!"

Jeremiah and the other four did as they were told, their faces pale by the light of the electric torches. The amber glowed and threw off its yellow fire.

The automatic spat flame, but Brad found the other's throat in his two hands.

Brad sprang to the head of the passage and started down, the pistol held before him, alert, ready for instant action. And action came, in the form of a stab of flame which sent lead whining off the stone wall. Brad fired at the flash and a scream echoed through the tunnel.

Dropping down on the floor, he waited for the second shot, and when it roared in his ears he took a second toll. Behind him the scientists were cringing against the wall, too frightened to move.

"Get down!" called Brad to the others. "Get down and crawl forward to me."

Rustling and the clink of amber told him that the five were obeying. He inched along the passage, waiting tensely for another shot.

He had nearly reached the turn in the tunnel when he placed his hand in something sticky and warm. The stench of blood, hot and salty, was in his nostrils, and it suddenly came to him with a shiver that he had taken human life.

But a shot, almost in his face, brought a grim tightness to his mouth. Calmly he raised the pistol, thrust it forward to feel it touch something yielding. His finger twitched and a shuddering body fell across his path.

The hot, sweet odor of smokeless powder was all about him as he crawled forward again. Far ahead he could see a glimmer of light, made by a hole in the floor above.

In back of him lay darkness, but ahead, between himself and the hole, he saw a shadow flicker across the passage. The pistol jumped back into his hand as it cast a round ribbon of flame down the passage. The shadow fell back and lay still.

Brad was deafened by the shots in close quarters. Grimly he wondered what he would find above ground, for he could hear no tramp of feet on the floor above.

The slap of leather beside him made Brad jump back. A rifle butt whistled past him and shattered itself against the stone wall, its crash echoed instantly by Brad's automatic.

Then, with the passage clear, and sending a call to the hovering men behind him, Brad ran up the passage to the dimly lighted hole. He could see nothing above it, but he jumped up and caught at the floor over his head. Something crushed at his fingers and he let go, to drop again into the tunnel.

"Drag some stones up here!" Brad commanded. "Pile them under this hole while I cover it."

The others asked no questions, did not even look at Brad, who stood with his pistol pointing at the hole. The stones were brought and piled up as directed.

Brad knew that he was taking a long chance, but he also knew that it was impossible to remain here, eventually to be starved out. These bandits—as they undoubtedly were—would stop at nothing to gain the hoard of amber which the expedition had so obligingly uncovered for them. And the loot of the Chang tombs was the one thing which stood between Jeremiah Williams and poverty. Without this amber, the entire expedition would be stranded in China, without the remotest possibility of obtaining funds.

With Brad, the circumstances were not so urgent. He was young and versatile. But with the others, who were old with their best work behind them, the amber was as vital as life itself.

The last stone was hoisted into place and Brad silently

crouched on top of the unsteady pile, ready to peer up over the edge and take what toll he could before he himself was shot. He held both his own and the officer's automatic in his hands.

Slowly he raised up until he was just beneath the opening. Then he suddenly sprang upright, his eyes blazing, his entire body as taut as a bowstring.

Two soldiers crouched just above him and he had no more than glimpsed their ugly faces when he fired point-blank. He whirled as a rifle spat flame at him. One of his pistols roared. The other rifle shot off his hat, and he replied with gunfire as he dodged back.

He saw that the dim room around him was vacant except for the two dead bodies, and he lost no time in scrambling up. Throwing down his empty pistols, he snatched up a rifle and bandolier.

"Come up!" He shouted into the hole. "It's clear!"

But it was not clear. Even before the last terror-stricken scientist had crawled out of the hole, rifle fire began to spit through the door, making the room tremble with the impact of hot lead.

Brad inched forward on the floor, shooting at random with the purloined rifle, hoping that at least some of his shots were taking effect.

Jeremiah suddenly shrieked, "Look out! They're above us!"

Brad rolled over and looked up. Through gaping cracks in the ceiling he could see men swarming in above them. Gray figures were running down the stairs. With a gasp, Brad realized that they had climbed up from the outside.

He was up in an instant, his rifle clubbed, running toward

the men at the bottom of the stairs. The roar was terrific. All attention was suddenly concentrated on Brad, for he alone was making a show of resistance.

Brad felt something sear his shoulder as he swung madly right and left with his gun. He felt the stock crashing down on bodies and heads, saw bayonets searching for him. He was surrounded and he swung the rifle in a wide arc. None of the Chinese bandits dared shoot for fear of hitting their own number. Time and again they attempted to dash in upon the lithe American, but the deadly curve of that rifle held them back.

Brad's arms were tiring from the repeated shock of his striking weapon. He saw a medley of faces about him, saw gray uniforms shifting giddily before him. Something engaged his gun and he felt it leave his hands. Then with a savage cry he hurled himself upon his attackers, his fists striking out at their faces.

The circle was closing on him, bearing him down. Above his head he saw a rifle begin to fall, and though it was the work of an instant, Brad felt that the dropping weapon came slowly. He tried to fend it off with his arms, felt the crash of wood against his wrist, saw it slip off and come directly at his head.

Sound and light exploded in his brain and he sank senseless to the stone floor, to be swallowed up immediately by the surge of Chinese above him.

The pain in his head and body was so great when he came to, that he could only stare up at the gray sky above, unable to understand the singsong Chinese which was being shouted around him. At last he marshaled his reeling senses sufficiently to gain an inkling of what was being said.

"Search them!" a voice commanded. "They will need nothing on their walk back to Peking."

Brad struggled to move, only to find that he was tightly bound, lying flat on his back amid the dead grass of the paving. He could see the towering pagodas against the lifeless sky and he was suddenly cold in the moaning north wind. Looking to one side, he saw the five scientists standing against a grotesque statue of a helmeted guard dog, their hands high as soldiers quickly removed everything of value from their clothing. The officer Brad had knocked out in the underground room was directing the procedure, a malicious smile on his ugly, misshapen face. He dangled the car keys in his hands.

Jeremiah Williams was shivering, his face ghastly in its terror. Not once did he glance toward Brad, though the youth lay directly in his line of sight.

"You are going to make us walk to Peking?" quavered Jeremiah, striving to enunciate his Chinese properly, though failing sadly.

"It will be good for you." The officer turned and saw that Brad had regained consciousness.

"Hah! Our little friend seems to be alive. That is well!" He strode over and kicked Brad harshly in the side.

Jeremiah was speaking again. "Then you do not intend to let us keep the amber?"

And in spite of his mingled emotions of pain and anger, Brad could scarcely restrain his smile at his uncle's show of misunderstanding.

"Why, of course!" replied the officer. "You have only to bring us the moon and we will gladly give it back to you." He laughed loudly and some of the soldiers smiled at their superior's wit.

It was not until then that Jeremiah gave the slightest thought to his nephew. "What are you going to do with the young man?"

The officer's smile was not nice to see. "He will remain as my guest, I am happy to say. You need not worry about ever seeing him again."

At last the search was done and the five white men were told to leave. Pointing fingers showed them the way to Peking, many miles across the hard, brown plain. They went fearfully, with never a backward glance, their legs trembling as though they felt bullets biting into their backs.

Horses were led up—square-faced Mongolian ponies, long-haired and as vicious as they were small. Two men lifted Brad up into a saddle where he swayed dizzily, his blue eyes dull with pain. Ropes were passed under the horse's belly and Brad felt himself bound tightly.

The Chinese officer stepped close to him. "Now we will have a pleasant afternoon ride, and perhaps tomorrow or the next day, you will pay for the lives you have taken." He smiled cruelly. "I myself will make you pay."

Brad could think of only one Chinese word in reply. "Pig!"

But the officer only smiled. He mounted another pony to lead the way north, deep into the frowning, mysterious Western Hills where only rumors live to account for the deaths of men.

As the cavalcade trotted through the tortuous canyons of the mountains, Brad lurched from side to side in the crude saddle, unable to brace himself. The wooden crosstrees bit alternately into his stomach and back, breaking the skin, and the leather cushion which was held down beneath him by a single strap seemed as sharp as broken glass.

They had progressed many miles when dusk found them, deep in the hills. The soldiers made a hasty camp and Brad was thrown heavily to the ground, to be staked down by cruelly tight ropes.

He lay awake through the long menacing night, cramped, cold and unable to move a muscle. When dawn came he breakfasted on a swallow of water, and was strapped again into the saddle.

Late in the afternoon they were winding through passes which were unbelievably twisted. The sharp backs of ridges jutted high above them against the gray sky, and the brown hillsides were steep and barren of vegetation.

At last, Brad saw a high wall before them which stretched east and west, following the ridges at their highest points. The wall was nearly thirty feet high and twenty feet broad. Dully, he recognized a section of the famed Great Wall of China.

But the Wall was not their goal, and they had just started the ascent to it when the officer in the lead swung to the west and entered a narrow, almost hidden pass. The ground beneath the horses' feet leveled out and looked as though it were much used. Brown shrubs grew above them on the steep sides of the cut, and ahead, as brown as the vegetation, Brad saw ramparts loom against the sky. He had little time to regard the silhouetted battlements, for a postern gate swung open and the cavalcade went through.

Brad found himself in a cobblestone courtyard, surrounded by frowning piles of masonry which were almost medieval in their architecture. A yellow-robed Manchurian came out to them, and in the yellow gown, Brad saw the answer to his wonderings.

He was within a lamasery of the Western Hills, one of those mysterious outposts of the lama religion. Through Brad's mind there coursed all that he had ever heard of these monasteries and their yellow-robed monks. He had heard much of their cruelty, but he remembered with burning vividness that no white man had ever lived to visit a lamasery in the Western Hills and return to tell about it.

Little time was given him for thought, however. Soldiers carried him across the courtyard, up a flight of steps and through a low doorway. As they carried him past an unobstructed section of the ramparts, Brad caught a glimpse of the Great Wall of China not far distant. He knew that it would thread its tortuous length down to the railroad through Nankou Pass, countless miles to the west.

The soldiers threw him into a cell and locked the door upon him, leaving him alone for the first time. They had loosened his bonds and now he worked strenuously to free himself.

He was standing up, stretching himself and feeling the ache of his whole body, when the gray-uniformed officer came to the door and stood silently regarding the American. The Chinaman ran critical eyes over the tall, lithe form and then looked into the rugged young face and laughed.

"It would be a shame," he remarked, "to allow you to die pleasantly. Tomorrow we will have a little sport. I am a very kind man. Very kind. I am about to offer you a challenge to a duel. You accept, of course?"

Brad did not answer. He stood motionless in the center of the cell, his feet wide apart, his hands on his hips, his eyes as cold as ice. The officer laughed again and then left.

Brad paced back and forth across the cell, listening to the sound of his boots ringing on the stone. There was clearly no way out of the cell, for the floor and sides were of stone and the door of strong iron.

The idea of the duel was equally clear. It was obvious that he would have no real fighting chance against the officer.

The night passed slowly, black and ominous. And at noon Brad found he had been right about being refused a fighting chance.

Armed guards bound his arms to his sides and made him walk out on the narrow wall. The entire monastery lay before him, a gloomy, rambling fortress of solid stone, relic of the days when Tartars were expected to sweep down across the Great Wall with the coming of each night.

Brad expected to be taken down to the courtyard below, but he found that the guards were forcing him up a flight of stairs which led to an even higher tower. A door opened before him and he found himself standing on the battlement-enclosed platform of the highest tower. Below were rocks hundreds of feet down, and the walls were almost sheer.

The Chinese officer and three men with yellow robes stood on the windswept tower, the cold air tugging at their clothing.

"Good afternoon," greeted the officer. "I see you are punctual in keeping engagements."

Brad had stopped, but a sharp bayonet at his back forced him on. He smiled coolly and looked about, faintly hoping that there might be some way of escape. But though the battlements were not as high as his knees, not even a fly could hope to scale the walls of the tower. The platform was several hundred feet in diameter and the only way of escape was at his back, guarded by armed soldiers.

The officer's face was ugly as he stepped toward Brad. Cruelty made his brown eyes beads in his puttylike face.

Then Brad knew what was about to happen. They would not untie his arms, nor would they give him any weapon. The officer was about to force him back to the edge, whipping at him with a keen sword, cutting him horribly until at last, from sheer desperation, the American would jump over the battlements to the waiting rocks far below.

The officer drew a sword and felt slowly of its keen edge, watching covertly to see if he had intimidated Brad. Then, playfully, the Chinaman thrust out with the keen blade and scraped Brad's chest. Involuntarily, the American stepped back, back toward the sheer wall and the embrasures.

The sword flickered out again, sending a hot pain through

Brad's arm. Again he stepped back, closer to the drop. He tried to free his arms of the confining ropes, but it was impossible to move them.

The ugly face in front of him smiled savagely, and light licked the keen blade. Brad took another step back, conscious of blood running down his right arm where the sword had touched. Out of the corner of his eye he saw that the lama priests were grinning viciously.

Brad felt the battlements at his heels and knew that he could step back no further. Seeing this, the officer stepped closer. His sword became a deadly, painful flash of light which darted relentlessly back and forth, biting into Brad's flesh.

But in his triumph, the Chinese officer failed to see that one stroke of the blade had cut the rope which bound Brad's arms to his sides. Brad felt his bonds loosen slightly, and though his chest was a hotbed of pain, he seized quickly upon a plan.

He pretended to step up on the raised embrasures, as though about to jump. Seeing this, the officer lunged forward to strike once more.

Brad doubled up, the blade swishing past his ear. Before the Chinaman could recover, Brad was under him, running across the platform toward the other side. The soldiers stood motionless, certain that this was merely an extension of the torture. The monks did not move.

The officer roared and ran swiftly after Brad, his heavy shoes ringing on the stones. The American turned at right angles, running along the circular wall, glancing back to see that the officer was close upon him. Brad twisted at his bonds and felt the rope leaving him.

Suddenly he turned and dived under the upraised sword, bringing his full weight against the running Chinaman. Surprise and fear were in the officer's bellow, because he saw that he was but a few feet away from the edge of the tower.

Brad encircled the man's legs with his free arms, throwing the officer off balance, feeling them both sway toward the edge. The sword came down, but too late.

Releasing his hold just in time, Brad threw himself back. The Chinaman pitched over the side, out of sight, to hurtle down to the waiting rocks.

Screams of the yellow-robed monks and shrill cries of the three soldiers were in Brad's ears as he jerked himself to his feet and turned. The smallest monk was only a few feet away and Brad lost no time. Not realizing the pain of his wounds, he jumped across to the lama before the man could move.

Snatching up the Chinaman, Brad held the man's light weight off the platform and ran toward the door. The soldiers were there, bayonets ready, though somewhat amazed at the sudden turn of events. But Brad did not pause in his headlong rush toward them. The bayonets came up viciously and two of them sank deep into the body of the lama priest. The third bayonet was thrust out, and before the soldier could recover Brad had felled him with a quick blow to the chin.

Diving through the door, he hurtled down the steps, passed the portal which led to the cell and ran further down into the tower. With cries close behind him, he swung down a long passageway which he saw led to a room.

A cluster of yellow robes was ahead of him and priests crouched tensely in the passage, waiting. But Brad, once started, knew no quarter or obstacle. With all the speed and grace of a football player, he hurtled in a flying tackle straight for the group.

Monks were bowled over like tenpins, and without a backward glance Brad was on his feet and pounding through the monastery.

His hurrying legs finally brought him into the ceremony rooms of the rambling structure and he found himself confronted with a life-sized Mongolian idol with pious hands beneath his chin. Brad almost rushed across the dimly lighted room to give combat when he realized where he was.

A lama monk was kneeling before the image in prayer when he felt himself snatched up, saw a fist crash into his face and dropped senseless.

Dragging the unconscious lama with him, Brad ran into the adjoining room. Another altar, lighted by the feeble glow of incense pots, loomed before him. The six hands of the image were variously posed, and the face was a woodenly placid mask. With his burden still in his hand, Brad stepped up before the idol.

Something moved to either side and he darted back. Two priests had been kneeling there. Brad's hands snatched out, caught hold of the robes and strove to batter the heads together. But, strangely, only a wooden thump met his effort. He kicked out and his boots found marks before the priests could raise a cry.

Kneeling down over the unconscious Manchurians, Brad discovered that they wore hideous carved and painted masks of tremendous size.

But the American lost no time in examinations. Feet were

pounding down a near corridor and Brad quickly dragged the three lamas into a small opening behind the hollow altar. As he passed the image a glitter, yellow as fire, caught his eye. With a gasp, he saw that the six hands were bedecked with the Chang amber which he had located at the tombs.

Cries lent him haste and he crouched down, rapidly binding and gagging his captives with strips torn from the yellow robes. One of the robes he saved, drawing it on over his own clothing, finding that it smelled of grease and sweat.

Safe momentarily in the dark niche, Brad took stock of his situation.

Though the sword cuts stung painfully beneath clotted blood, he realized he was very hungry.

Hours passed and he knew that it must be dark outside. Searching parties had passed through the room several times, but they had been hasty and had failed to look behind the idol.

Brad started to get to his feet and felt one of the masks under his hand. He picked it up, seeing by the faint light that it was black and plumed, much larger than a human head. The face was a twisted horror. Without a second thought, Brad drew it on over his tawny hair and adjusted it until he could see through the eyeholes.

Then, sedately, his yellow robes dragging about him, the mask heavy on his shoulders, he made his way out of his hiding place and stepped up to the altar. Quickly denuding the image of the glittering amber, placing the invaluable relics in a hastily constructed bag of yellow cloth, he stepped out of the room and found a stairway which seemed to lead down.

Two lamas passed him on the stairs, gave him a puzzled

glance and then nodded. Brad calmly returned the nod and swept majestically by. He knew that masks must be out of place elsewhere in the monastery, but he prayed for luck and found himself stepping through a doorway which led into the courtyard.

The hoofs of a pony rang out on the cobblestones, and by the light of a lantern hanging over the door, Brad saw a soldier riding toward him, in the direction of the postern gate. As the horseman entered the light, Brad raised himself up on the balls of his feet and prepared for a spring.

With a startled exclamation, the soldier was hurled to the ground, and before he could rise again, Brad was up on the horse in a swirl of yellow robes. The startled pony bucked and then ran forward.

Cries of alarm split the night and lights appeared on every side. Straining his eyes through the suddenly peopled darkness, Brad saw that the postern gate was open. With his robes streaming, grotesque in his mask, he leaned low over the horse's neck and beat his heels against the pony's flanks. A soldier was in the act of shutting the postern, but Brad swung the bag of amber over his head and smashed it into his face.

Then he was out of the lamasery, leaving bedlam behind him. Throwing off the cumbersome mask, Brad put the horse through the cut at breakneck speed. The way he had entered would probably be blocked, so he hit upon a daring plan.

At the end of the cut he turned and forced the pony up the steep hillside to the base of the Great Wall. He knew that this broad highway might place him in Nankou where he could catch a train for Peking, and he prayed for luck.

The Great Wall reared up above him and he raced along its side. Torches were flaring behind him, and above the drumming of the pony's hoofs on the hard ground, he could hear the shouts of his pursuers.

Then he glimpsed a spot blacker than the wall and he pulled up short, forcing the pony through a door in the mammoth structure. Dismounting, he threw off his yellow robe and quickly felt for the stairway he knew must be there. He found it and led the unwilling horse upward.

He was on top of the wall, mounting again, when a volley of shots screamed past his head as soldiers drew rein beside the door.

Even paving was under him as he raced along the twenty-foot highway. Then stairs caused his horse to stop sharply. With a glance back, to see that his example had been emulated, Brad whipped the pony down a flight of steps twenty feet wide and hundreds of feet long.

The soldiers breasted the stairway and fired wildly at the dim horseman below them. Seeing that their firing had no effect, they spurred down.

The Wall shot up at unexpected angles, twisted and turned, dived steeply down. In places it was crumbled and the going was rough, but for the greater part, it was passable. Here, where the Tartars had been so long held at bay, Brad was racing with death and fortune.

The night was ominous and full of strange cries. And then suddenly as he forced the fleet pony along, Brad saw the night gape emptily before him through a watchtower, saw that the mad onrush of his horse could not be stopped!

At the risk of broken limbs, he swung off at full speed! His horse screamed as it plunged down, to land a hundred feet below.

Caught by an embrasure, Brad struggled dazedly to his feet and looked back. The soldiers were almost upon him. Looking down, he saw that the Wall abruptly stopped in thin air and began again in the face of a solid cliff far down.

Praying that he had not been seen, Brad clutched his precious sack of amber and slipped into the watchtower, tensely listening to the hoofbeats rushing toward him. And the mounted soldiers did not pause in their pursuit, knowing no more of this deserted section of the Wall than Brad had known. Suddenly the two in the lead saw the drop and screamed, trying vainly to halt their ponies. But above the roll of hoofs, the others had not heard the warning and they crashed into their leaders.

Brad saw the soldiers crash down into emptiness, heard the impact of writhing bodies on the rocks below.

Two men had managed to pull up in time and they stood, frozen with terror, staring over the fatal drop.

Brad, in the shadows, snapped, "Hands high! Move and I shoot!" His weaponless hands trembled as he strove to make his Chinese clear. "Drop your guns and dismount!"

Still dazed from the horror they had just witnessed, the soldiers dismounted slowly. Their guns clattered to their feet.

"Walk toward me!" ordered Brad.

The soldiers obeyed and when they were a safe distance away from their guns, Brad leaped out of the shadows, hands clenched. He struck out, and felt one man go down.

The other soldier had seen the weaponless hands and he sprang for Brad's throat. Weaving back, Brad struck him deftly in the stomach and followed it up with a quick right to the jaw. The soldier slumped back and fell heavily.

Securing the Chinamen loosely, that they might escape later, Brad caught one of the horses and picked up a rifle. Retracing his steps along the Wall, he found a stairway leading down to the China side.

Five hours later, with dawn breaking over the Western Hills, Brad arrived at Nankou to take a train for Peking. He was a sadly bedraggled and bloody figure, fatigued and hungry, when he boarded the train.

But the service of the railroad amended most of his difficulties, and when he took a rickshaw from the station and sent the boy pattering along toward the hotel, he was somewhat rested and a little less ragged.

His uncle was in his suite with the other four men when Brad arrived. Striding into the room, Brad flung the yellow sack to the table.

Looking amusedly at the open mouths of the five men, Brad remarked, "There's your loot. I hope my delay in getting it for you didn't cause you any concern."

Jeremiah Williams gave his nephew a severe glance. "Why, of course not, Brad."

He cleared his throat noisily and snatched up some of the amber, fingering it hungrily. "Of course not, Brad. In fact, we thank you very much."

STORY PREVIEW

NOW that you've just ventured through some of the captivating tales in the Stories from the Golden Age collection by L. Ron Hubbard, turn the page and enjoy a preview of *Golden Hell*. Join Captain Humbert Reynolds when he travels to Mongolia seeking gold, only to be captured and tortured by bandits. At their mercy and condemned to work deep within the bowels of a Mongolian mine, Reynolds must lead a daring against-all-odds escape or face certain death.

Golden Hell

ONE night in the Hotel du Pekin, a man uttered a statement which was to sentence me to more hardship and privation than I had ever before known, and to more danger, and to more high adventure than I had thought possible in this commonplace world.

Leaning on the bar and looking at me bleary-eyed, Charlie Martin said, "*All* Mongolians are rich."

Not much, but enough. Why were they rich? Certainly it wasn't commerce and it wasn't agriculture. That nomadic people, now that I came to think of it, had no visible means of support and yet—THEY WERE ALL RICH.

I am not what you'd call a romantic adventurer, neither an adventurer nor romantic. I don't happen to like the sound of either. What I've done has come under the head of experience and perhaps exploit and sometimes conquest. You might even call me hardheaded, determined to get what I want where I want it—and that, to my everlasting sorrow, is not a fitting or a fit code for any man.

I know all these things now and I didn't then. I know entirely too much how wrong I was. I've seen things since that night in the Hotel du Pekin which even now I can't believe I have seen. But the mental scars are there.

Had you asked me, there at the bar, "Do you believe in

God?" I would have replied, "Well, yes and no," and in a bigoted way I would have explained a very complex conception to you. Now, to the same question, I would say, "I don't know. I've never had any great proof of God. But I know there's a hell. LOST UP THERE IN THE GOBI, I FOUND IT!"

In a careless way, you've heard men say, "I went to hell and back to get that." They didn't mean hell, really.

But I do.

This gold beside me, that diamond in this ring. I went to hell and brought them back.

Up there, lost in the Gobi, there's a mountain with a name so sacred to Mongols that even here I dare not write it. Why? Because that mountain has a festering wound in the craggy side, and through that wound, men pass on their journey to hell.

Charlie Martin knew a lot about such things. He was an archaeologist attached to a museum and he looked at all things in a sober, academic light. He went on to expound his theory of why Mongolians were all rich and it was too common for repetition.

As I parted with him that night, my mind was already dwelling on a wild idea which had come to me. I said, in a careless sort of way, "I think I'll take a run up to Kalgan and maybe beyond in a few days."

"Country's pretty wild right now," said Charlie. "Watch yourself."

I would have done very well to have heeded his advice, but I didn't. I was too immersed in this idea of mine.

All Mongolians were rich and they didn't have mines. But the Gobi was a big place and who knew what you could find in those flat-topped scarps which rose like a child's blocks out of the gravelly waste.

Two days later I was on my way. Thanks to Charlie, I had a letter to the Prince of East Sung, a man very influential in the country, and I anticipated no difficulties.

You see, simple fool that I am, I thought that there would be gold up there, and if there was, what would hinder my scouting around, finding it and staking out a claim? I had a small gasoline-driven, dry panner with which to test those gravelly washes where no water ever flowed.

Gold is a driving force. It had taken me on a wild trek through the country of the ancient Mayas until the Yucatán Indians had driven me out. It had taken me through the upper forgotten mountains of Ecuador, and through the endless wilderness of northern Canada. I knew gold, but little else. I had a degree in mining, but the soberer jobs left me cold. I always managed to make my stake and keep going, nothing terribly rich, but enough. A mining engineer, when he takes the prospector's trail, doesn't experience very much difficulty. He can pass the old sourdoughs with their odd ideas and he can guess at things the so-called practical miner never suspects exist.

Young and confident, full of plans and enthusiasm, I arrived at the palace of the Prince of East Sung. The place was imposing, as yellow as the great plains and the Golden Mountains, built like a fort, ancient beyond the count of years. You had the impression of frowning dignity.

At the gate I was met by a cavalry officer, a fellow who bulked in his bursting furs like some overstuffed sack and whose head sat upon that mountain of flesh like some pagoda upon a mountain peak. He was slit-eyed, well greased, yellow and watchful. His fingers itched for the bribe I gave him. His name was Yang T'ang, a crazy singsong thing.

He escorted me into the presence of the Prince.

The Prince of East Sung was a very young man with a smooth yellow complexion, more Chinese than Mongol. He wore a beautifully embroidered blue gown and a small round cap and a pair of cavalry boots with golden spurs. He leaned back in his massive blackwood chair as though too weary to even think about moving.

"You have come," he said in a bored voice, "for my protection. You cannot have it."

I had not spoken and his refusal of a request I had not thought to make took me off balance.

"I am here," he continued in Oxford English, "because my ancestors were here. But my subjects desert me and join me at will. I have a personal bodyguard but the cavalry you have seen is not mine; the cavalry only wishes my protection for the moment and attaches allegiance to me only as long as they think they need my support. So do not ask for aid, *Tou-kie.*"

He was not being encouraging. He had called me "foreign dog." But it sounded so odd, those drawling broad A's coming from that mouth, I could not help but smile. "So doah not ahwsk foah aid."

From my pocket I produced a hundred dollars in Bank of Taiwan notes. I laid it respectfully upon the dais. He glanced at it and then at the captain who had brought me in. The captain was licking fitfully at his gross lips.

"That is better," said the Prince. "Since you request nothing, I will give you the escort. The country, I might add, is dangerous. But what do you want? Old bones?"

Incautiously, I said, "Gold."

He sat up stiff as a poker, staring. "Gold? Here in Mongolia? *Tou-kie,* you are a fool among fools. Go back to Peking and forget about this thing."

"No, you do not understand," I insisted. "I merely wish to try out the old streambeds of the region, to prospect that which has not been touched before. I take no wealth from the people, but from the land where it has lain forgotten."

"Escort him out, Yang T'ang," said the Prince with a disgusted wave of his hand. "Think well about this, *Tou-kie,* or you may find gold."

That was not encouragement, as I found out later. That was a threat, a threat more ugly than any I would ever hear again. He had, with that remark, sentenced me.

To find out more about *Golden Hell* and how you can obtain your copy, go to www.goldenagestories.com.

GLOSSARY

STORIES FROM THE GOLDEN AGE *reflect the words and expressions used in the 1930s and 1940s, adding unique flavor and authenticity to the tales. While a character's speech may often reflect regional origins, it also can convey attitudes common in the day. So that readers can better grasp such cultural and historical terms, uncommon words or expressions of the era, the following glossary has been provided.*

---

aileron: a hinged flap on the trailing edge of an aircraft wing, used to control banking movements.

altimeter: a gauge that measures altitude.

archy gunners: antiaircraft gunners; World War I British slang that probably derives from the arched pattern of the antiaircraft projectile trajectory.

bandolier: a broad belt worn over the shoulder by soldiers and having a number of small loops or pockets for holding cartridges.

barrel rolled: having executed a barrel roll, a flight maneuver where the aircraft has completed a rotation on its longitudinal axis while approximately maintaining its original direction.

batteries: groups of large-caliber weapons used for combined action.

bull fiddle: also called a bass fiddle or double bass; the largest and lowest-pitched string instrument, and member of the violin family. It has a deep range, going as low as three octaves below middle C.

Canton: city and port in the southern part of China, northwest of Hong Kong.

casqued: having a military headpiece or helmet on.

Chang tombs: also known as the Ming tombs, the imperial cemetery located near Peking. The building of the first tomb, Chang Lang, or tomb of Chang, was begun by the third emperor of the Ming Dynasty in 1409 AD before the main peak of Tian Shou Mountain, which means "heavenly longevity." The area contains the tombs of thirteen emperors, twenty-three empresses and a number of concubines, princes and princesses.

Chapei: a poor residential district of Shanghai, China, which was bombed by the Japanese in 1932 following a skirmish with Chinese troops. A number of innocent civilians were killed, which roused international concern.

C-in-C: Commander in Chief.

club: airplane propeller.

cordite: a family of smokeless propellants, developed and produced in the United Kingdom from the late nineteenth century to replace gunpowder as a military propellant for large weapons, such as tank guns, artillery and naval guns. Cordite is now obsolete and no longer produced.

cowl: a removable metal covering for an engine, especially an aircraft engine.

crate: an airplane.

crosstree: the raised wooden pieces at the front and rear of the saddle that form a high pommel or horn in the front and cantle in the back.

drew rein: from "draw in the reins," meaning to slow down or stop by exerting pressure on the reins.

embrasure: the low segment of the alternating high and low segments of a battlement along the outer top of a wall or tower, through which weapons may be fired.

Fen Ho River: an eastern tributary of the Yellow River in the Shan Province in northern China, approximately 435 miles (700 km) long. The Fen River valley was an early center of civilization and has remained an important route linking Peking with the Shan Province, and with the major land routes to Central Asia.

file closer: a commissioned or non-commissioned officer in the rear of a line, or on the flank of a column, who rectifies mistakes and ensures steadiness in the ranks.

fire step: a step cut into the wall of a trench some two or three feet from the floor that runs along the entire wall. The purpose was to enable each occupant of the trench to peer over the side in the direction of the enemy. The floor of the trench was lower than the fire step so that men could pass along the trench without exposing their heads to enemy fire.

General Chang: Chang Hsüeh-liang (1901–2001); nicknamed "Young Marshal," he became the military governor of

Manchuria after the assassination of his father, a major warlord of China, by the Japanese in 1928. He was made vice commander in chief of all Chinese forces and a member of the central political council. He made historic contributions to ending the ten-year (1927–1937) civil war, helping realize the cooperation between the Nationalist regime and the Communist Party of China, and making the whole nation take part in the war of resistance against Japanese aggression.

G-men: government men; agents of the Federal Bureau of Investigation.

Gobi: Asia's largest desert, located in China and southern Mongolia.

Golden Mountains: also known as the Altay Mountains; "Altay" means "Mountains of Gold" in Mongolian. The mountains are located in Central Asia where Russia, China and Mongolia come together.

Harbin: the capital and largest city of Heilongjiang Province, in northeastern China.

Hawks: bomber aircraft.

Hotel du Pekin: in the 1930s it was considered one of the finest hotels in the Orient. Built in 1917, the hotel had 200 rooms with baths, a tea hall with nightly dancing and its own orchestra for classical dinner music. It also had a spacious roof garden overlooking the Forbidden City and the Legation Quarter (walled city within the city exclusively for foreigners).

ideographs: written symbols that represent an idea or object directly, rather than by particular words or speech sounds, as Chinese or Japanese characters.

jury strut: a strut that keeps an aircraft's wings from bowing or snapping when air pressure pushes down on them.

Kalgan: a city in northeast China near the Great Wall that served as both a commercial and a military center. Kalgan means "gate in a barrier" or "frontier" in Mongolian. It is the eastern entry into China from Inner Mongolia.

key: a hand-operated device used to transmit Morse code messages.

Khinghan Mountains: forested volcanic mountains extending 700 miles (1,126 km) along the eastern edge of the Mongolian Plateau (large plateau including the Gobi Desert) in western Manchuria. The mountains slope gently from the west, reaching moderate elevations of only 2,000 to 3,000 feet (610 to 915 meters).

Manchuria: a region of northeast China comprising the modern-day provinces of Heilongjiang, Jilin and Liaoning. It was the homeland of the Manchu people, who conquered China in the seventeenth century, and was hotly contested by the Russians and the Japanese in the late nineteenth and early twentieth centuries. Chinese Communists gained control of the area in 1948.

Mayas: a member of a group of Indian peoples, chiefly of Yucatán, Belize and Guatemala, whose languages are Mayan.

Mukden: the capital city of the China province of Liaoning in northeast China.

mushed: flown in a partly or nearly stalled condition.

Nankou: a city located northeast of Peking, near the Great Wall.

Nankou Pass: a large gap in the mountains that connects China with Mongolia and along which the Great Wall was built. Through this pass flowed all the vast volume of trade and travel between China and Mongolia. It was through here that the barbaric Mongols for centuries poured their armies to invade and devastate the plains and cities of China. It was to stop these dreaded invasions that the Great Wall was built.

panner: a container in which gold, or other heavy and valuable metal, is separated from gravel or other substances by agitation.

Peking: now Beijing, China.

pointer's ledge: seat located on the left side of the gun breech for the pointer to sit on. The pointer is the gun crew member who points the artillery piece and fires the weapon.

postern: postern gate; small secondary entrance, sometimes concealed, and usually at the rear of a castle or fortress, used as a means to come and go without being seen or as a route of escape.

QST: radio signal meaning "general call to all stations." The Q code is a standardized collection of three-letter message encodings, all starting with the letter "Q"; initially developed for commercial radiotelegraph communication and later adopted by other radio services.

quarterdeck: the rear part of the upper deck of a ship, usually reserved for officers.

route step: a normal pace in marching in which it is not necessary to march in step. Used mainly in the field when moving from place to place as a unit.

rudders: devices used to steer aircraft. A rudder is a flat plane or sheet of material attached with hinges to the craft's stern or tail. In typical aircraft, pedals operate rudders via mechanical linkages.

Scheherazade: the female narrator of *The Arabian Nights*, who during one thousand and one adventurous nights saved her life by entertaining her husband, the king, with stories.

seventy-five or **75:** 75 mm field artillery piece, first introduced in 1897.

Shanghai: city of eastern China at the mouth of the Yangtze River, and the largest city in the country. Shanghai was opened to foreign trade by treaty in 1842 and quickly prospered. France, Great Britain and the United States all held large concessions (rights to use land granted by a government) in the city until the early twentieth century.

Shan Province: also known as *Shanxi, Shan-hsi* or *Shansi;* province of northern China. The name *Shanxi* means "west of the mountains," derived from its location west of the Taihang Mountains. It serves as a buffer between China and the Mongolian steppes and was a key route for military and trading expeditions. It was also one of the major avenues for the entrance of Buddhism into China from India.

Shen Province: also known as *Shensi* or *Shaanxi;* north central province neighboring Shan Province.

sideslip: (of an aircraft when excessively banked) to slide sideways, toward the center of the curve described in turning.

sourdoughs: settlers or prospectors, especially in the western United States or northwest Canada and Alaska.

struts: supports for a structure such as an aircraft wing, roof or bridge.

Taiy: also known as Tai-yuan; the capital of Shan Province.

Tartars: members of any of the various tribes, chiefly Mongolian and Turkish, who, originally under the leadership of Genghis Khan, overran Asia and much of eastern Europe in the Middle Ages. Also the descendants of these people.

trace: trace-chain; a chain used to connect the limber (a two-wheeled, horse-drawn carriage that holds the cannon) to a horse's harness.

tracer: a bullet or shell whose course is made visible by a trail of flames or smoke, used to assist in aiming.

USN: United States Navy.

Wagon-Lit: name of a hotel. *Wagon-Lit* means "sleeping car" in French. Sleeping compartments on trains were first introduced by Georges Nagelmackers in 1872 to service international railroad travelers on trains such as the Orient Express. The original company, Campaignie Internationale des Wagons-Lits, later expanded into hotels.

Wei River: river in north central China. It flows east through Shan Province to join the Yellow River. It is 537 miles (864 km) long. Its valley was the earliest center of Chinese civilization and until the tenth century AD was the site of a succession of capital cities. In the third century BC, the area around the junction of the Ching and Wei rivers was the site of the first ambitious irrigation works in China.

Western Hills: a range of hills in China, situated northwest of Peking, which contains structures from the Ming and Qing dynasties and has forests of pine and fir trees. The range is known for its many temples and has long been a religious retreat. It also serves as a retreat for Chinese scholars and members of the government and civil service.

white man's burden: from a poem written by Rudyard Kipling originally published in 1899 with regard to the US conquest of the Philippines and other former Spanish colonies. Subject to different interpretations, it was latched onto by imperialists to justify colonialism as a noble enterprise. Much of Kipling's other writings suggested that he genuinely believed in the benevolent role that the introduction of Western ideas could play in lifting non-Western peoples out of "poverty and ignorance."

White Russian: a Russian who fought against the Bolsheviks (Russian Communist Party) in the Russian Revolution, and fought against the Red Army during the Russian Civil War from 1918 to 1921.

windsock: a fabric tube or cone attached at one end to the top of a pole to show which way the wind is blowing.

windward: facing the wind or on the side facing the wind.

Yucatán: a peninsula mostly in southeastern Mexico between the Caribbean Sea and the Gulf of Mexico.

L. Ron Hubbard
in the Golden Age
of Pulp Fiction

*In writing an adventure story
a writer has to know that he is adventuring
for a lot of people who cannot.
The writer has to take them here and there
about the globe and show them
excitement and love and realism.
As long as that writer is living the part of an
adventurer when he is hammering
the keys, he is succeeding with his story.*

*Adventuring is a state of mind.
If you adventure through life, you have a
good chance to be a success on paper.*

*Adventure doesn't mean globe-trotting,
exactly, and it doesn't mean great deeds.
Adventuring is like art.
You have to live it to make it real.*

— *L. RON HUBBARD*

L. Ron Hubbard
and American
Pulp Fiction

B ORN March 13, 1911, L. Ron Hubbard lived a life at least as expansive as the stories with which he enthralled a hundred million readers through a fifty-year career.

Originally hailing from Tilden, Nebraska, he spent his formative years in a classically rugged Montana, replete with the cowpunchers, lawmen and desperadoes who would later people his Wild West adventures. And lest anyone imagine those adventures were drawn from vicarious experience, he was not only breaking broncs at a tender age, he was also among the few whites ever admitted into Blackfoot society as a bona fide blood brother. While if only to round out an otherwise rough and tumble youth, his mother was that rarity of her time—a thoroughly educated woman—who introduced her son to the classics of Occidental literature even before his seventh birthday.

But as any dedicated L. Ron Hubbard reader will attest, his world extended far beyond Montana. In point of fact, and as the son of a United States naval officer, by the age of eighteen he had traveled over a quarter of a million miles. Included therein were three Pacific crossings to a then still mysterious Asia, where he ran with the likes of Her British Majesty's agent-in-place

L. Ron Hubbard, left, at Congressional Airport, Washington, DC, 1931, with members of George Washington University flying club.

for North China, and the last in the line of Royal Magicians from the court of Kublai Khan. For the record, L. Ron Hubbard was also among the first Westerners to gain admittance to forbidden Tibetan monasteries below Manchuria, and his photographs of China's Great Wall long graced American geography texts.

Upon his return to the United States and a hasty completion of his interrupted high school education, the young Ron Hubbard entered George Washington University. There, as fans of his aerial adventures may have heard, he earned his wings as a pioneering barnstormer at the dawn of American aviation. He also earned a place in free-flight record books for the longest sustained flight above Chicago. Moreover, as a roving reporter for *Sportsman Pilot* (featuring his first professionally penned articles), he further helped inspire a generation of pilots who would take America to world airpower.

Immediately beyond his sophomore year, Ron embarked on the first of his famed ethnological expeditions, initially to then untrammeled Caribbean shores (descriptions of which would later fill a whole series of West Indies mystery-thrillers). That the Puerto Rican interior would also figure into the future of Ron Hubbard stories was likewise no accident. For in addition to cultural studies of the island, a 1932–33

LRH expedition is rightly remembered as conducting the first complete mineralogical survey of a Puerto Rico under United States jurisdiction.

There was many another adventure along this vein: As a lifetime member of the famed Explorers Club, L. Ron Hubbard charted North Pacific waters with the first shipboard radio direction finder, and so pioneered a long-range navigation system universally employed until the late twentieth century. While not to put too fine an edge on it, he also held a rare Master Mariner's license to pilot any vessel, of any tonnage in any ocean.

Yet lest we stray too far afield, there is an LRH note at this juncture in his saga, and it reads in part:

"I started out writing for the pulps, writing the best I knew, writing for every mag on the stands, slanting as well as I could."

To which one might add: His earliest submissions date from the summer of 1934, and included tales drawn from true-to-life Asian adventures, with characters roughly modeled on British/American intelligence operatives he had known in Shanghai. His early Westerns were similarly peppered with details drawn from personal experience. Although therein lay a first hard lesson from the often cruel world of the pulps. His first Westerns were soundly rejected as lacking the authenticity of a Max Brand yarn

Capt. L. Ron Hubbard in Ketchikan, Alaska, 1940, on his Alaskan Radio Experimental Expedition, the first of three voyages conducted under the Explorers Club flag.

(a particularly frustrating comment given L. Ron Hubbard's Westerns came straight from his Montana homeland, while Max Brand was a mediocre New York poet named Frederick Schiller Faust, who turned out implausible six-shooter tales from the terrace of an Italian villa).

Nevertheless, and needless to say, L. Ron Hubbard persevered and soon earned a reputation as among the most publishable names in pulp fiction, with a ninety percent placement rate of first-draft manuscripts. He was also among the most prolific, averaging between seventy and a hundred thousand words a month. Hence the rumors that L. Ron Hubbard had redesigned a typewriter for faster keyboard action and pounded out manuscripts on a continuous roll of butcher paper to save the precious seconds it took to insert a single sheet of paper into manual typewriters of the day.

That all L. Ron Hubbard stories did not run beneath said byline is yet another aspect of pulp fiction lore. That is, as publishers periodically rejected manuscripts from top-drawer authors if only to avoid paying top dollar, L. Ron Hubbard and company just as frequently replied with submissions under various pseudonyms. In Ron's case, the

---

A MAN OF MANY NAMES

Between 1934 and 1950, L. Ron Hubbard authored more than fifteen million words of fiction in more than two hundred classic publications. To supply his fans and editors with stories across an array of genres and pulp titles, he adopted fifteen pseudonyms in addition to his already renowned L. Ron Hubbard byline.

Winchester Remington Colt
Lt. Jonathan Daly
Capt. Charles Gordon
Capt. L. Ron Hubbard
Bernard Hubbel
Michael Keith
Rene Lafayette
Legionnaire 148
Legionnaire 14830
Ken Martin
Scott Morgan
Lt. Scott Morgan
Kurt von Rachen
Barry Randolph
Capt. Humbert Reynolds

list included: Rene Lafayette, Captain Charles Gordon, Lt. Scott Morgan and the notorious Kurt von Rachen—supposedly on the lam for a murder rap, while hammering out two-fisted prose in Argentina. The point: While L. Ron Hubbard as Ken Martin spun stories of Southeast Asian intrigue, LRH as Barry Randolph authored tales of

romance on the Western range—which, stretching between a dozen genres is how he came to stand among the two hundred elite authors providing close to a million tales through the glory days of American Pulp Fiction.

L. Ron Hubbard, circa 1930, at the outset of a literary career that would finally span half a century.

In evidence of exactly that, by 1936 L. Ron Hubbard was literally leading pulp fiction's elite as president of New York's American Fiction Guild. Members included a veritable pulp hall of fame: Lester "Doc Savage" Dent, Walter "The Shadow" Gibson, and the legendary Dashiell Hammett—to cite but a few.

Also in evidence of just where L. Ron Hubbard stood within his first two years on the American pulp circuit: By the spring of 1937, he was ensconced in Hollywood, adopting a Caribbean thriller for Columbia Pictures, remembered today as *The Secret of Treasure Island.* Comprising fifteen thirty-minute episodes, the L. Ron Hubbard screenplay led to the most profitable matinée serial in Hollywood history. In accord with Hollywood culture, he was thereafter continually called upon

The 1937 Secret of Treasure Island, *a fifteen-episode serial adapted for the screen by L. Ron Hubbard from his novel,* Murder at Pirate Castle.

to rewrite/doctor scripts—most famously for long-time friend and fellow adventurer Clark Gable.

In the interim—and herein lies another distinctive chapter of the L. Ron Hubbard story—he continually worked to open Pulp Kingdom gates to up-and-coming authors. Or, for that matter, anyone who wished to write. It was a fairly unconventional stance, as markets were already thin and competition razor sharp. But the fact remains, it was an L. Ron Hubbard hallmark that he vehemently lobbied on behalf of young authors—regularly supplying instructional articles to trade journals, guest-lecturing to short story classes at George Washington University and Harvard, and even founding his own creative writing competition. It was established in 1940, dubbed the Golden Pen, and guaranteed winners both New York representation and publication in *Argosy*.

But it was John W. Campbell Jr.'s *Astounding Science Fiction* that finally proved the most memorable LRH vehicle. While every fan of L. Ron Hubbard's galactic epics undoubtedly knows the story, it nonetheless bears repeating: By late 1938, the pulp publishing magnate of Street & Smith was determined to revamp *Astounding Science Fiction* for broader readership. In particular, senior editorial director F. Orlin Tremaine called for stories with a stronger *human element*. When acting editor John W. Campbell balked, preferring his spaceship-driven tales, Tremaine enlisted Hubbard. Hubbard, in turn, replied with the genre's first truly *character-driven* works, wherein heroes are pitted not against bug-eyed monsters but the mystery and majesty of deep space itself—and thus was launched the Golden Age of Science Fiction.

The names alone are enough to quicken the pulse of any science fiction aficionado, including LRH friend and protégé, Robert Heinlein, Isaac Asimov, A. E. van Vogt and Ray Bradbury. Moreover, when coupled with LRH stories of fantasy, we further come to what's rightly been described as the foundation of every modern tale of horror: L. Ron Hubbard's immortal *Fear*. It was rightly proclaimed by Stephen King as one of the very few works to genuinely warrant that overworked term "classic"—as in: *"This is a classic tale of creeping, surreal menace and horror. . . . This is one of the really, really good ones."*

To accommodate the greater body of L. Ron Hubbard fantasies, Street & Smith inaugurated *Unknown*—a classic pulp if there ever was one, and wherein readers were soon thrilling to the likes of *Typewriter in the Sky* and *Slaves of Sleep* of which Frederik Pohl would declare: *"There are bits and pieces from Ron's work that became part of the language in ways that very few other writers managed."*

L. Ron Hubbard, 1948, among fellow science fiction luminaries at the World Science Fiction Convention in Toronto.

And, indeed, at J. W. Campbell Jr.'s insistence, Ron was regularly drawing on themes from the Arabian Nights and

so introducing readers to a world of genies, jinn, Aladdin and
Sinbad—all of which, of course, continue to float through
cultural mythology to this day.

At least as influential in terms of post-apocalypse stories was
L. Ron Hubbard's 1940 *Final Blackout*. Generally acclaimed
as the finest anti-war novel of the decade and among the
ten best works of the genre ever authored—here, too, was a
tale that would live on in ways few other writers imagined.

Hence, the later Robert Heinlein
verdict: "Final Blackout *is as perfect
a piece of science fiction as has ever
been written."*

Like many another who both
lived and wrote American pulp
adventure, the war proved a tragic
end to Ron's sojourn in the pulps.
He served with distinction in four
theaters and was highly decorated

*Portland,
Oregon, 1943;
L. Ron Hubbard,
captain of the
US Navy subchaser
PC 815.*

for commanding corvettes in the North Pacific. He
was also grievously wounded in combat, lost many a
close friend and colleague and thus resolved to say
farewell to pulp fiction and devote himself to what it
had supported these many years—namely, his serious research.

But in no way was the LRH literary saga at an end, for
as he wrote some thirty years later, in 1980:

*"Recently there came a period when I had little to do. This
was novel in a life so crammed with busy years, and I decided to
amuse myself by writing a novel that was* pure *science fiction."*

That work was *Battlefield Earth: A Saga of the Year 3000*. It was an immediate *New York Times* bestseller and, in fact, the first international science fiction blockbuster in decades. It was not, however, L. Ron Hubbard's magnum opus, as that distinction is generally reserved for his next and final work: The 1.2 million word *Mission Earth*.

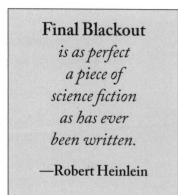

Final Blackout *is as perfect a piece of science fiction as has ever been written.*

—Robert Heinlein

How he managed those 1.2 million words in just over twelve months is yet another piece of the L. Ron Hubbard legend. But the fact remains, he did indeed author a ten-volume *dekalogy* that lives in publishing history for the fact that each and every volume of the series was also a *New York Times* bestseller.

Moreover, as subsequent generations discovered L. Ron Hubbard through republished works and novelizations of his screenplays, the mere fact of his name on a cover signaled an international bestseller. . . . Until, to date, sales of his works exceed hundreds of millions, and he otherwise remains among the most enduring and widely read authors in literary history. Although as a final word on the tales of L. Ron Hubbard, perhaps it's enough to simply reiterate what editors told readers in the glory days of American Pulp Fiction:

He writes the way he does, brothers, because he's been there, seen it and done it!

THE STORIES FROM THE GOLDEN AGE

Your ticket to adventure starts here with the Stories from
the Golden Age collection by master storyteller L. Ron Hubbard.
These gripping tales are set in a kaleidoscope of exotic locales and brim
with fascinating characters, including some of the
most vile villains, dangerous dames and brazen heroes
you'll ever get to meet.

The entire collection of over one hundred and fifty stories is being
released in a series of eighty books and audiobooks.
For an up-to-date listing of available titles,
go to www.goldenagestories.com.

AIR ADVENTURE

Arctic Wings	*Man-Killers of the Air*
The Battling Pilot	*On Blazing Wings*
Boomerang Bomber	*Red Death Over China*
The Crate Killer	*Sabotage in the Sky*
The Dive Bomber	*Sky Birds Dare!*
Forbidden Gold	*The Sky-Crasher*
Hurtling Wings	*Trouble on His Wings*
The Lieutenant Takes the Sky	*Wings Over Ethiopia*

FAR-FLUNG ADVENTURE

SEA ADVENTURE

TALES FROM THE ORIENT

MYSTERY

FANTASY

SCIENCE FICTION

WESTERN

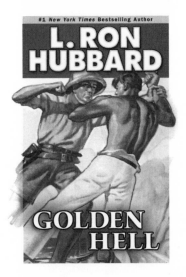